A MAN IN THE

WHEATFIELD «

To Becky,

This Author is one of Nevada's favorite sons; this story one of his finest

Jon

BOOKS BY ROBERT LAXALT

*The Violent Land: Tales the Old Timers Tell*

*Sweet Promised Land*

*A Man in the Wheatfield*

*Nevada*

*In a Hundred Graves: A Basque Portrait*

*Nevada: A Bicentennial History*

*The Basque Hotel*

*A Time We Knew: Images of Yesterday in the Basque Homeland*

*Child of the Holy Ghost*

*A Lean Year and Other Stories*

*Dust Devils*

*A Private War: An American Code Officer in the Belgian Congo*

*The Land of My Fathers: A Son's Return to the Basque County*

*Time of the Rabies*

*Travels with My Royal: A Memoir of the Writing Life*

# A MAN IN THE WHEATFIELD

by Robert Laxalt

Foreword by Cheryll Glotfelty

UNIVERSITY OF NEVADA PRESS
RENO & LAS VEGAS

*A Man in the Wheatfield*, by Robert Laxalt, was originally published in 1964 by Harper & Row, Publishers, Inc. of New York, Evanston, and London. The present volume reproduces the first edition except for addition of a foreword and changes made to the title and copyright pages to reflect the new publisher.

University of Nevada Press, Reno, Nevada 89557 USA
Copyright © 1964 by Robert Laxalt
Foreword copyright © 2002 by the University of Nevada Press
All rights reserved
Manufactured in the United States of America
Cover design by Carrie House
Library of Congress Cataloging-in-Publication Data
Laxalt, Robert, 1923–2001
A man in the wheatfield / by Robert Laxalt ; foreword by
Cheryll Glotfelty. — University of Nevada Press pbk. ed.
p. cm.
ISBN 0-87417-521-6 (alk. paper)
1. Italian Americans—Fiction. 2. Rattlesnakes—Fiction.
3. Strangers—Fiction. 4. Villages—Fiction. 5. Nevada—Fiction.
6. Clergy—Fiction. I. Title.
PS3562.A9525M3 2002
813'.54—dc21    2002008815

The paper used in this book meets the requirements of American National Standard for Information Sciences—Permanence of Paper for Printed Library Materials, ANSI Z39.48-1984. Binding materials were selected for strength and durability.

University of Nevada Press Paperback Edition, 2002
FIRST PRINTING
11 10 09 08 07 06 05 04 03 02    5 4 3 2 1

FOR JOYCE

# Foreword

THE DAY THAT ROBERT LAXALT, AGE seventy-seven, departed this world, March 23, 2001, was a sad day for Nevada. For fifty years Nevadans had enjoyed the writing of this gifted native son—in Laxalt's early newspaper articles, which covered topics as varied as Carson City politics, gas chamber deaths, and mobsters at Lake Tahoe; in magazine articles and short stories set in what he termed "The Other Nevada," vignettes about rural communities, buckaroos, and sheepherders of the sagebrush hinterland; and, most memorably, in Laxalt's seventeen books that ranged widely in genre and geography, from short stories about the Old West to a family portrait of the Old World, from state histories of Nevada to a novel about Basque smugglers in the Pyrenees, and from a coming-of-age love story between a young cowboy and an Indian maiden to a riveting memoir about serving as a code officer in what was then the Belgian Congo during World War II. Laxalt could always be counted on to tell a good story, to get it right, and to leave the reader feeling uplifted by the beauty of language, charmed by arresting images, and ennobled by his greatness of soul.

Robert Laxalt's memorial service at the University of Nevada, Reno, was a veritable Who's Who of Nevada, featuring eloquent tributes from Governor Kenny Guinn, former university president Joe Crowley, poet Shaun Griffin, the late newspaper-mogul Rollan Melton, Monsignor Leo McFadden, former chairman of the Nevada Gaming Control Board Alan Abner, journalism professor Warren Lerude, and Laxalt's three distinguished children, attorneys Monique and Bruce and doctor Kristin. Fittingly, the ceremony began with a Basque song entitled "Agur Jaunak" ("Greetings Gentlemen") and ended with a traditional Basque honor dance, the Auresku. Perhaps the greatest homage, however, was the crowded auditorium itself, representing a tremendous gathering of readers who had been personally touched by Laxalt's words.

The man whose life was celebrated that day was born in 1923 to Theresa and Dominique Laxalt, Basque immigrants who came to America to start a new life. Like so many Basque immigrants to the American West, Dominique became a sheepherder. When the money from this venture proved inadequate to Theresa's ambitions for the family, she opened up a hotel in Carson City, where Robert Laxalt and his five siblings spent their early years. As a boy, Robert contracted a near-fatal case of rheumatic fever that kept him bedridden for months. It was at this time that Robert became an avid reader, feeding the mind of the future writer. Determined to regain his physical strength, Laxalt became a formidable boxer as a youth. He attended a Jesuit college, Santa

Clara University, for two years before serving in World War II. Laxalt completed his college degree at the University of Nevada, Reno, where he fell in love with Joyce Nielsen. The newlyweds soon had three children, and Robert, sobered by his new responsibility as paterfamilias, became a news reporter, started his own news bureau, became a staff correspondent for United Press International, and eventually took the more stable job of director of news and publications at the University of Nevada, Reno. During his entire news-reporting and university careers, Laxalt wrote prodigiously on the side, often in the wee hours of the morning while his family slept, contributing articles to *National Geographic, The Atlantic Monthly, Saturday Evening Post, Cosmopolitan, Reader's Digest,* and others, and eventually becoming most renowned for his books.

Laxalt was named Distinguished Nevada Author in 1982 by the Friends of the University Libraries, and in 1988 became the first inductee to the Nevada Writers Hall of Fame. His first national book, *Sweet Promised Land*—an affectionate story of his father's immigration to America as a young man, life as a shepherd in the uncrowded landscapes of the West, and eventual realization that Nevada had become more of a home to him than his Basque Country homeland—was published by Harper and Row in 1957 and became a best-seller that has never gone out of print and that spawned numerous annual Basque festivals throughout the American West. Laxalt is internationally known for his writing about Basque people, culture, and history. He received one of Spain's most prestigious literary honors, the Tambor de Oro, for his novel *A Cup of Tea in Pamplona.* His literary style has often been likened to Hemingway's, and his themes are universal.

Laxalt's first two books were published by Harper and Row and were widely reviewed and critically acclaimed. All his later works were published by the University of Nevada Press, which he helped to establish in 1961 and directed until 1983. While Robert Laxalt enjoys a local and international reputation, he deserves and would surely have garnered a much greater *national* following had he stayed with a major East Coast trade press rather than switching to a small West Coast academic press. One hopes that Laxalt's loyalty and generosity to the University of Nevada Press will be rewarded in the end, as the press he founded and shepherded for more than twenty years keeps his books in print—alive—where they may continue to reach new readers.

For those familiar with Laxalt's writing, *A Man in the Wheatfield* stands out as conspicuously as, well, a man standing in a wheatfield. While stylistically the novel is vintage Laxalt, it seems strikingly different from his other works in its subject matter and tone. *Sweet Promised Land,* published seven years earlier than *A Man in the Wheatfield,* is more characteristic of Laxalt's work as a whole. Like *Sweet Promised Land,* most of Laxalt's work—fiction and nonfiction—draws from the experiences of himself and his family. *The Basque Hotel,* for example, is an autobiographical novel centering on Laxalt's boyhood in the small state capital of Carson City, Nevada, during Prohibition and the Great Depression. Although given fictional names, characters in *The Basque Hotel* are readily identifiable, based on real-life models. Similarly, *Child of the Holy Ghost* traces the story of Laxalt's mother, while *The Governor's Mansion* follows the intense family involvement in the political campaigns of Robert's brother Paul, who served one term as Nevada's governor and two terms as U.S. senator. While Laxalt's Basque-family trilogy explores aspects of the Basque-American experience, several other books—*In a Hundred Graves, A Cup of Tea in Pamplona,* and *A Time We Knew*—are set in the Basque Country near the border of Spain and France and explore aspects of Basque culture, character, and history. Yet another frequent subject of Laxalt's writing is his home state of Nevada, about which he has written two histories and numerous articles. Where, then, does *A Man in the Wheatfield* fit in Laxalt's work? It is not about his family, it is not about Basques, it is not historical, and it is not even obviously set in Nevada—no places are named at all in the novel. Where did *A Man in the Wheatfield* come from, and how does it relate to Laxalt's other work?

While *A Man in the Wheatfield* may appear to be pure fiction, with no autobiographical elements, Laxalt's wife, Joyce, believes that it is his *most* autobiographical work. "You get the closest sense of Bob in this book than anywhere else," she contends. And where is Laxalt to be found in the book? Surprisingly enough, in one of the least likable characters in the novel—the priest, Father Savio Lazzaroni. As Laxalt reveals in his memoir, *Travels with My Royal,* in childhood he had been terrified by a recurring nightmare of "an unknown and unseen presence of evil" (148). In *A Man in the Wheatfield* this childhood dream takes the shape of a door opening into a little attic room in which another door opens onto terrifying darkness in which Lazzaroni is struck by an unseen presence—"the thing was monstrous and black upon black" (9). Joyce Laxalt recalls that the house where Laxalt grew up did have an attic room, which, even as an adult, Robert refused to show her. Lazzaroni's second dream, which he began having as a seminary student, also mirrors a dream that tormented Robert Laxalt since his days at the Jesuit college. In this dream, the unknown presence in the child's nightmare has taken on the shape of a man standing in a wheatfield. The man is dressed in a black suit and black hat, but Lazzaroni cannot make out the man's face.

This recurring nightmare likely had its origins in Laxalt's strict Catholic upbringing, where he was taught that God was to be feared and that evil was not an abstract concept but, rather, a living presence. *A Man in the Wheatfield* proved to be Laxalt's way of exorcizing his own demons. As he recalls in *Travels with My Royal,* when the book was finished, "my own devils dematerialized, evaporated under the harsh light of written exposition. I've never had either dream since" (149–50). Laxalt recalled to a reporter in 1979, "It was a very painful book to write. The story was very close to me. At that time I felt that evil was a separate, active force in the world" (Smith). As Laxalt battled his way into the dark unknown, Joyce recalls how he would write at the top of a page, "What in hell are you trying to say?" The book was begun in the attic of a rented villa in the Pyrenees mountains, while the Laxalt family was on a one-year stay in the Basque Country in 1960–61, during which Laxalt served as a Fulbright Research Fellow and consultant to the Library of Congress on Basque culture. The family had spent some months on the seacoast at Saint-Jean-de-Luz, France, and were en route to their next destination when they stopped to enjoy a local festival. Their car was burglarized, and a footlocker containing the manuscript of a novel-in-progress about Basques in America was stolen. A year-and-a-half's work disappeared in one afternoon, and Laxalt was left in despair, unable to reconstruct the novel from memory. Out of his misery was born the dark novel that is *A Man in the Wheatfield*. In retrospect, Laxalt felt it to be a "much more important book" than the purloined one (*Travels* 147).

The snakes. Where did Laxalt get the book's central symbol and image? In a blend of symbolism and realism that marks the book itself, it is likely that Laxalt's snake imagery stems both from the biblical serpent in Genesis and from the rattlesnake collection of a snake handler whom Laxalt met in Dayton, Nevada, a small town along the Carson River, on which the unnamed town in the novel is loosely based (Joyce Laxalt). This man and his snakes became the germinating idea for Laxalt's short story "The Snake Pen," which years later metamorphosed into *A Man in the Wheatfield*. In "The Snake Pen," Smale Calder, a mechanic, marries a local farm girl named Jenny. He has a snake pit, and his handling of the snakes seems to drain his libido, such that Jenny grows sexually frustrated to the point where she seduces one of her father's hired hands. A local boy sneaks into the snake pen and dies, and a county sheriff dispatches all the snakes with a shotgun. Without his snakes, Calder's sex drive returns with a vengeance, and Jenny loses weight under the fierce power of his nightly passion. Then one day, Jenny spots a rattlesnake in their yard and pleads with Calder to kill it. He reassures her that he "got rid of him." Strangely, though, Calder's sex drive diminishes again, and Jenny grows restless once more. One night, after Calder has collapsed into bed, Jenny sneaks into his garage, where she discovers the rattlesnake in a wire cage.

The last line of the story reads, "She was terribly frightened, but she did not know why" ("Snake" 181). Readers will have no difficulty identifying the differences between "The Snake Pen" and *A Man in the Wheatfield*, and doing so highlights the evolution of an idea in the mind of an artist.

It is one thing to have an idea, of course, and quite another to find a publisher for it. "The Snake Pen," in fact, was rejected by popular magazines, with comments such as "snakes are practically automatically out" (*Lean* xii). One of the more thoughtful rejection letters warned Laxalt, "I am afraid that you have repeated yourself in moiling about in topics which tend to be effective as literary tour de force, but almost impossible to think of in a commercial sense. . . . THE SNAKE PEN is a damn good story, . . . but my candid opinion is that you must turn your talents to more digestible backgrounds if you would succeed financially in your writing" (*Lean* xii).[1] While the rejected story confronted the reader with a dozen pages of rattlesnakes, the new novel fixated on them for nearly two hundred pages. Thus, despite the huge success of *Sweet Promised Land*, the acceptance of this new manuscript was by no means assured.

If you go upstairs to the main library at the University of Nevada, Reno, pass through the Business and Government Information Center, and proceed down a narrow hallway, you will reach the door to the Special Collections Department. If you then peruse the twenty-four file boxes of Robert Laxalt Papers, you may discover a treasure. It is a plain white piece of typing paper with a penciled note: "Bruce & Nick & Kris— I wanted you to know. Harpers has taken the book. Isn't that wonderful—. Poppa." One imagines that Robert Laxalt left this note on the dining room table for his children to find when they woke up in the morning or came home from school in the afternoon. They would have known that the book was their father's first novel, that he had struggled with its composition, and that for several suspenseful months he had been anxiously waiting to hear back from Harper and Row. Considering the literary establishment's fear of snakes, there was good reason to celebrate Harper's acceptance and, likewise, ample cause to wonder what the reviewers would say.

The novel examines what happens to the people of a small, isolated town when an outsider moves in. Viewed from the surrounding hills, the town is shaped like "an imperfect star in the desert . . . as though a master hand had dropped a splash of green paint on an immense and barren canvas and the paint had run on out to its uncertain ends to form the star shape" (1). The town was established by an Italian immigrant named Manuel Cafferata during the Depression of the 1930s on the site of an abandoned mining town in the American West. For Cafferata, who had driven out to the desert to commit suicide, the town offered a new chance, and he built it up by inviting other Italian immigrants to join him, supplemented by new recruits from Italy. Cafferata became the unelected mayor, creating a town patterned on an Old World village, complete with baker, butcher, barber, banker, bartender, restaurateur, mechanic, priest, and farmers. All went well during the days of the town's growth, but now, in the years following World War II, "there were only embers of the old life, . . . everyone was tired" (21), and "the town was dying" (17). Enter an "American" named Smale Calder, who, unbeknownst to Cafferata, bought the local gas station and garage. Calder's individualism and desire to be left alone goes against the style of the tightly knit community and causes resentment. When it is learned that Calder keeps rattlesnakes as pets, the fears latent in the villagers are revealed, and the changes incipient in the town manifest themselves.

The shape of the narrative resembles the wheel of a covered wagon, with Calder and his snakes at the hub and each surrounding character developed along the spoke of his or her relationship to that central figure; the inexorable turning of that wheel of human relationships propels the destiny of everyone comprising it. For Cafferata, unable to control either Calder or the villagers' response to him, Calder's arrival spells the end of his waning power. For the priest, Calder precipitates a spiritual crisis in which he confronts the evil he has feared all his life and realizes that it lies within himself. For other minor characters, Calder likewise serves as a catalyst, eliciting their fears, desires, and virtues. Laxalt's shifting point of view allows the reader to follow the thoughts and actions of these characters as they each confront their own worst enemy—themselves.

The snakes are at once characters in their own right and master symbols as Laxalt achieves an unusual blend of the literal—diamondback rattlesnakes in the high desert of the American West—and the figurative—the serpent in the Garden of Eden. Are they evil? Father Lazzaroni believes that they are, but Laxalt, reflecting on the book in *Travels with My Royal*, replies, "Of course not. They are used here as a Christian symbol. In Grecian times, the house snake was holy. In this story, snakes are the innocents of life" (155). The snakes, then, are both themselves and whatever we believe them to be. To Calder they are "the most beautiful things on God's earth" (*Man* 167). To other characters they represent variously a public danger, a Sunday's entertainment, a profitable tourist attraction, private property, an embodiment of lust, and the life force of Calder himself. To no one are the snakes simply snakes, devoid of special significance. In this novel Laxalt explores, elaborates, and, finally, explodes the age-old human proclivity to turn the snake into a symbol.

Compared to the insights we get into the hearts of the principal characters Cafferata and Lazzaroni and peripheral characters such as Tony, Amado, Luigi, Tosca, Della Santa, and others, Calder himself, like his snakes, remains somewhat of a cipher, an unknown man psychologically. It is as if Calder is a mirror that reflects the insides of the other characters but is himself to be known only from the outside by his actions and utterances. To be sure, our own personal reactions to Calder and his snakes may teach us something about ourselves. The priest, in the end, regards Calder as "his first pure human being, without guise and without fear, as beautiful in his simplicity and as ugly as the very snakes he loved" (*Man* 168). Laxalt in *Travels with My Royal* calls Calder "an innocent, natural man," who "brings out hidden emotions in the people. Innocence unfortunately does this. . . . Humanity does not like innocence. People mistrust it. . . . Mankind will kill innocence. I wish that I could believe otherwise" (*Travels* 152, 153, 155).

Laxalt's discussion of *A Man in the Wheatfield* in his memoir offers a retrospective reading of the book, written nearly four decades after its original publication. From this vantage point, Laxalt can say, xviii §

    I realize now that while I was writing this book, I was exploring for myself the meanings of such overused words as *good, envy, ego, hypocrisy, innocence, symbol, myth*.

    We all know the meanings of these words. . . . And like all the meanings of words describing the human condition, we don't know them at all, until we have to discover them all over again for ourselves.

    This book was my exploration. (*Travels* 149)

While Laxalt's retrospective view illuminates the achievement of the novel, a letter that he wrote to his editor at Harper and Row before the book was accepted helps to explain his intent. In response to questions that Elizabeth Lawrence raised about the manuscript, Laxalt replied,

> You are right in seeing it as a parable. But it is my own concept of a parable, grounded in reality with people and ideas in realistic conflict, because to my mind, the perfect parable is not acceptable in the cynical, practical world of now.
>
> Beneath the surface story of conflict, I saw it as innocence caught up between the opposing forces of spiritualism, as depicted by the priest, and the practical, as shown by the politician. . . .
>
> Because [Calder] is an innocent and an individual allied with no one, he becomes the whim of everybody and is inevitably destroyed. . . .
>
> The story turns on two things—fear and compassion. Fear in the sense that evil springs from it, and they are confused and intertwined. Compassion, or understanding in the deepest sense of the word, as the opening of

vision to see past evil to the fear that motivates it. . . . The cycle will repeat itself in another place and circumstance, as it always has.

How well were Laxalt's intentions for this book realized? Did reviewers see in it what Laxalt had in mind? As the reviews rolled in from around the country Laxalt was very pleased that they were overwhelmingly positive. With catchy titles such as "Truth Is a Snake," "The Evil Is Within," "Of Good and Evil and Man and Snake," "An American Desert Parable Soaks Up Tragedy," "Exploring Ancient Shadows," "Symbols in Spare Prose," and "Satan Visits Small Town, or Does He?" the reviews described the novel in terms close to Laxalt's own, one reviewer calling it "both allegory and morality play about the nature of evil and fear," another, a "short parable . . . concerned with good and evil and the confusion between them," and another, "a parable concealing and revealing fear and prejudice which corrupt innocence and separate brothers" (*Books of the Southwest*; Rackemann; William). Reviewers identified the theme of the novel as, in one review, "the nature of evil, man's reaction to it and man's growing consciousness of himself in relation to it," and in another, "men's various ways of confronting fear and the presence of death" (William; "Truth"). Reviewers praised Laxalt for a style they described as "spare, forthright," "Hemingway-clean," "lean," "understated," like "a sword, of high-grade steel, two-edged," and "as stripped down and sun-bleached as the desert itself" (Rackemann; Bulla; *Books of the Southwest*; Etulain; William; "Truth"). One reviewer noted that "Laxalt has chiseled out a narrative that is lapidary, unadorned and original" ("Truth"). Some reviewers lapsed into snake language, one reviewer describing the townspeople's reactions to the snakes as "envenomed," another noting that the priest fastens his hostility to its object with "a reptilian deadliness," and another concluding that Laxalt "succeeds powerfully in creating a novel that leaves in the mind a sense of truth lying in wait, with a dry rustle, coiled to strike" ("Truth"; Bell; "Truth").

Among the reviews there were a few detractors, one regretting that "the allegory came first and the people followed," another that Laxalt on occasion "slips into direct explanation," another objecting to "the loose use of viewpoint, invading . . . the minds of several characters in a chapter," and still others finding the snake symbolism heavy-handed, one critic, in a review titled "Loaded with Chaff," accusing Laxalt of "symbololatry" (Tigue; "Truth"; Tigue; "Loaded"). For many readers, however, these possible weaknesses are inseparable from the novel's strengths—its timelessness, universality, clarity, and intensity. Indeed, *A Man in the Wheatfield* has been one of Robert Laxalt's most successful books. It was runner-up in the $10,000 Harper-novel contest, was named one of six notable works of fiction for 1964 by the American Library Association (along with Saul Bellow and a posthumous work by Ernest Hemingway), was reprinted in Great Britain and made available in a Spanish-language edition in Spain and South America, was optioned several times for film, and was reprinted by the University of Nevada Press in 1987. One reviewer, noting the 1957 publication date of *Sweet Promised Land*, concluded, "Laxalt appears to be a born writer. Let us hope we don't have to wait another seven years for his next book," a hope that Laxalt himself surely must have shared (Lawrence).

Indeed, what is remarkable about *A Man in the Wheatfield* is the compression and focus the novel achieves in spite of the centrifugal pull of the many different demands on Laxalt's time and energy during this period. The power and emotional intensity of the novel are reminiscent of Dostoyevsky or Kafka, and one might readily surmise that this short work was written in a single, uninterrupted burst of creative genius, perhaps—if one's imagination goes a little wild—with Laxalt's food and water being delivered on a tray placed on the floor outside his garret door. Nothing could be further from the truth. The manuscript was laboriously composed over a two-year period, started in the Basque Country in France and concluded back home in Reno, Nevada, where Laxalt maintained a more than full-time job at the university, responsible for all publications, including the university catalog, alumni magazine, and news releases. On top of this, Laxalt served as director of the newly established University of Nevada Press. Add to his university work Laxalt's responsibilities to his own family, plus heavy involvement in the political campaigns of his brother Paul, and you have a life so fragmented and taxing that it must have taken an extraordinary exertion of will to complete this novel, which was all the more difficult as it dealt with personally threatening material. Laxalt's close friend and fellow Nevada writer, Walter Van Tilburg Clark, would commiserate in a letter written just after the novel had been accepted, "I know very well, out of quite different but equally distracting circumstances, how hard it is to find just the time, let alone the mind and feeling and continuity, to write anything of one's own in the midst of the full time demands of what has to be regarded as the #1 job." Behind *A Man in the Wheatfield* loomed a man behind a typewriter, struggling against formidable odds to bring this dark brainchild to light. That Laxalt did press on to the finish reveals much about his own character.

*A Man in the Wheatfield* struck a chord with American readers in 1964, in the midst of the Cold War, when fear of communism created paranoia on a national scale, and when the West and the East were cast in terms of good and evil. Calder's effect on the town was described on the book's dust jacket as being "like a bombshell," employing the vocabulary of the intensive nuclear testing taking place in America—in Nevada, specifically—during this era. But while the book that explored fear and evil certainly had a Cold War timeliness, it also possessed truths that transcended the historical moment. One reviewer saw the book as exploring "man's *eternal* prejudice and his unreasoning fear of those things alien to him," and another identified its theme as being "the nature of man in *all* times and places" (Bosworth; Bell—my emphases). *A Man in the Wheatfield* also speaks to us, citizens of the new millennium. In the wake of September 11, 2001, with the War on Terrorism in full swing and a new federal Office of Homeland Security installed, with the words *good* and *evil* once more being deployed by a United States president and propagated through the media, the eternal issues that Laxalt struggles to explore for himself are very much, once more, our issues, as they will always be.

CHERYLL GLOTFELTY
*University of Nevada, Reno*
*March 23, 2002*

## NOTE

1. "The Snake Pen" was published for the first time in *A Lean Year and Other Stories* (Reno: U of Nevada P, 1994), a collection of published and unpublished stories from Laxalt's early writing years.

## WORKS CITED

Bell, Millicent. "The Evil is Within." Rev. of *A Man in the Wheatfield,* by Robert Laxalt. *New York Times,* 25 Oct. 1964.

Bosworth, J. Allan. "Exploring Ancient Shadows." Rev. of *A Man in the Wheatfield,* by Robert Laxalt. *Virginian Pilot,* Norfolk, Va., 29 Nov. 1964.

Bulla, Marilyn. "Symbols in Spare Prose." Rev. of *A Man in the Wheatfield,* by Robert Laxalt. *Observer,* Raleigh, N.C., 25 Oct. 1964.

Clark, Walter Van Tilburg. Letter to Robert Laxalt. 14 November 1963. Robert Laxalt Papers. Special Collections Department, University of Nevada, Reno.

Etulain, Richard W. Rev. of *A Man in the Wheatfield,* by Robert Laxalt. *Highroller* 24.4 (Oct./Dec. 1987).

French, Winsor. "Of Good and Evil and Man and Snake." Rev. of *A Man in the Wheatfield,* by Robert Laxalt. *Press,* Cleveland, Ohio, 11 Dec. 1964.

Jordan, Jenice. "Satan Visits Small Town, Or Does He?" Rev. of *A Man in the Wheatfield,* by Robert Laxalt. *Dispatch,* Columbus, Ohio, 10 Jan. 1965.

Lawrence, Wes. "An American Desert Parable Soaks Up Tragedy." Rev. of *A Man in the Wheatfield,* by Robert Laxalt. *The Plain Dealer,* Cleveland, Ohio, 18 Nov. 1964.

Laxalt, Joyce. Personal interview. 22 February 2002.

Laxalt, Robert. Letter to Elizabeth Lawrence. 27 September 1963. Robert Laxalt Papers. Special Collections Department, University of Nevada, Reno.

———. *A Man in the Wheatfield*. New York: Harper & Row, 1964. Rpt. Reno: U of Nevada P, 1987.

———. "The Snake Pen." *A Lean Year and Other Stories*. Reno: U of Nevada P, 1994. 169–81.

———. *Travels with My Royal: A Memoir of the Writing Life*. Reno: U of Nevada P, 2001.

"Loaded with Chaff." Rev. of *A Man in the Wheatfield*, by Robert Laxalt. *Book Week; New York Herald Tribune; Washington Post; San Francisco Examiner*, 15 Nov. 1964.

Rackemann, Adelaide C. "New Novel by Robert Laxalt." Rev. of *A Man in the Wheatfield*, by Robert Laxalt. *Sun*, Baltimore, Maryland, 8 Nov. 1964.

Rev. of *A Man in the Wheatfield*, by Robert Laxalt. *Books of the Southwest* n. 350, January 1988.

Smith, Roger. "*A Man in the Wheatfield* is News Again." *Gazette, Journal*, Reno, Nev., 26 Aug. 1979: 1B.

Tigue, Ethel E. "Distracting Technique Aids Novel's Climax." Rev. of *A Man in the Wheatfield*, by Robert Laxalt. *Tribune*, Minneapolis, Minn., 7 Feb. 1965.

"Truth is a Snake." Rev. of *A Man in the Wheatfield*, by Robert Laxalt. *Time*, 13 Nov. 1964.

William, Sister Mary. Rev. of *A Man in the Wheatfield*, by Robert Laxalt. *Best Sellers*, Scranton, Pennsylvania, 1 Nov. 1964.

# A MAN IN THE WHEATFIELD ⋘

# 1

It was in fact Father Savio Lazzaroni who in his despair looked down upon the little town and saw that it was an imperfect star in the desert. From where he stood in meditation on the hill, it was as though a master hand had dropped a splash of green paint on an immense and barren canvas and the paint had run on out to its uncertain ends to form the star shape.

Later he had mentioned it by chance to Manuel Cafferata, whose town it was. The idea had pleased Cafferata's fancy, though not in the sense that the priest had meant it. But then, whenever Father Savio said anything of this nature, Cafferata seemed always to hear with different ears and take out of it only what he wanted.

The kind of god that Manuel Cafferata liked to play was not of the Olympian who looks down on things below, else he would have thought to mount to the little hill from the beginning. But when the fact was called to his attention, it intrigued him enough to make the climb on foot to the top of the hill, puffing against the buttoned bind of his black

## 2 §

vest and with sweat dripping from the ends of his drenched mustache.

Once he was there, he could see that the tiny cluster of stone buildings and the surrounding fields did indeed make a certain star shape, if one stretched his imagination a little. And he could see how the accident had come to be. The river that flowed from the far Sierra widened briefly in the hollow that was the town, as if in a last show of strength before it struggled on to sink and die in the desert. It was from this hollow that the farmers drew their water, forcing it upward as they found good soil. And the good soil had been found in broad swaths that narrowed as they reached farther away. Here and there, however, the fields were irregular and getting more so with new plantings that pushed sideways. Joe Caneva's new alfalfa field had almost joined two of the star points, and something would have to be done about that.

Manuel Cafferata did not recover his senses until he had spoken to Joe Caneva about it, and Caneva had looked at him as if he were a fool, to think that a man would give up good soil for something like a star. After that, Cafferata risked no more hurts to his standing with impractical visions about the shape of the town. The only lesson he learned was one that he had already known, that it was for other kinds of men to climb to high places and see visions in the things that better men before them had built, not with dreams, but with work. But even as he said this to himself, he felt a whisper far back that told him this had always been his lacking, that if he had had a little of this other kind of man

## 3 §

in him, he could have arranged many of the big things in his life better from the beginning, instead of waiting until it was almost too late to do anything about it.

It had been a long time since he had felt this whisper, and perhaps what had made it come back was climbing to the top of the little hill. He had stood there with head uncovered under the blazing sun and the arch of the blue sky, while the desert air dried his perspiration. As on another day so long ago that it seemed like another life, his nostrils had been filled with the pungency of the summer sagebrush, and the only sounds he could hear in the great silence were the pounding labors of his heart and the whistle of his breath.

But in the time before, these sounds had not seeped from an overstuffed belly and tired lungs but had sprung from a young body in the constrictions of fear. He could see the road he had taken from the railroad town that was the county seat, beyond the range of gray desert hills. It was graded now, but still unpaved, and it followed almost the same route as the dirt road over which he had bounced in the steaming old wreck of a car he had put together with his own hands. A wreck of a car and a wreck of a shotgun that did not even belong to him, and a man fleeing from the company of other sallow-faced and hopeless men who lived with acrid fumes and sooty houses and bad wine and sad music, on the wreck of impossible dreams already forgotten. Because he believed himself to be a man above other men, he had not dreamed but expected, and so could not forget what America had promised him. When his presuming cost

## 4 §

him the only thing of self-respect he had left, his job when jobs were impossible to come by, there was not much else he could have done than what he tried to do.

In the open desert, though, he found out why it was that men killed themselves in dank woodsheds. When he had started out, it had been an easy thing to do. He had attached absolutely no importance to it at all. No arranging of his mind was required, no courage and no purpose. He had been born, such and such a thing had happened to bring him where he was, and such and such a thing was about to happen. It was simply that he had been traveling a long and dark road downward, and had come to the natural end of it.

But in the white glare of the desert and the eternity of silence and, mostly, the sun heat that had been working its way relentlessly into his soul-dead body, he had begun to feel a flickering of what he had set out to do. And when he realized he had made a fatal error in going out into the desert for no other reason than that it seemed necessary to die away from the others, panic had taken him. With his head swinging from side to side like an animal, he had searched for a place to hide from the sun. The old car had careened crazily across the desert, as much out of the road as in.

He had seen the abandoned cluster of tumbling stone buildings as a man dying of thirst would see water. The blackness of an open doorway yawned up into his swimming vision, and he had jerked the car to a stop. To stop was all that was in his mind, and he had not even turned off the motor, but lunged for the shotgun and clambered over the side of the door. There was a thick growth of weeds and sagebrush between him and the doorway, and the first thing

## 5 §

that happened was that the gun got tangled up and he had to tear it loose from the twisting tentacles. Then, when he began to run again, the mud that was clinging to his feet caught him up so that he pitched head and chest into it. He had floundered almost to his feet and slipped and fallen again, and the second time, he had lain prone in the mud while his heaving breath turned to sobbing rage against the conspiracy and, finally, to the healing tears of a child.

After a long time in which he had begun to be aware that the motor of the car was still running, he got up as far his knees. He had started to brush the mud from his hands when, in an absent memory of movement from a time before, he felt the grain of the mud and began to work it between his fingers. The smell of wet soil rose up around him. He raised his eyes and saw the crumbling gray stone of buildings that were like the stone houses of his boyhood and, finally, the blue sky and the hot sun.

In a while, he had gotten to his feet and gone to the road and turned off the motor of the old car. He stood leaning against it, his arms crossed on his chest. Something was growing inside him, quietly and without emotion, because he would never in his lifetime know emotion fully again. As much as a man who has been in war, he had passed over the abyss twice, once in going and once in returning, and he had left part of his soul on the other side, robbed from him forever by its touch with death.

In that moment, he had seen the ruin of buildings, but he had not seen the ruin of the hopes of the men who had built them. He saw only stone. He had seen the river and the rude, protruding skeletons of rockers and waterwheels covered with the silt that a great flood had brought to the bottom land in a day long past, but he had not seen the doom of that day. He saw only water and rich soil. Sun and stone and soil and water and, in time beyond, bountiful fields of green and gold, and farmhouses and a town, and the sounds of women with their market baskets visiting in the street and black-haired men with faces burned deep red talking with passion over wine glasses in the saloon.

And at last, the beginning he had been promised, a chance for the taking if a man were willing to work for it. Then, for the first time, he had gripped himself with his hands and felt his forgotten strength.

Father Savio Lazzaroni was in one respect different from the most of men, or for that matter, the most of priests. He knew for a positive fact there was a devil.

It had nothing to do with his training for the priesthood, which had left enough latitude to conceive of the devil in many ways. It was a certain knowledge with him, so that he could allow himself to think about it only at the right times. Because if it were not the right time, he felt that by thinking about it he could actually invoke a physical presence. It was a thought that sent him pale and shaken to his knees, groping for the dispelling arms of prayer.

His knowledge of the devil had come from two dreams in his life. One had been the dream of a child and the other the dream of a man. And it was precisely because of this that he had never been able to talk to anyone about it, because who, after all, really believed in dreams. He had even gone through that dissection himself for no other reason

## 7 §

than to ridicule what was growing into a certainty within him. But every time he did, the dream returned in what he began to realize in horror was a reminder, as if a studied intelligence unknown to him had ordered it.

He could clearly remember when he had first dreamed the dream as a child, and long afterward he would say to himself, *It began that night, and I can remember that it did.* But then, in an unguarded moment, it would come to him that the dream went back much further, that it had been with him always, that it had come into the world with him. The dream that he remembered was merely the first time it had revealed itself.

He had been a child, and he lay in a child's bed. The room was dark, but there was a window by his bed, and by the pale light from the night outside he had been watching the patterns in the lace curtain. He must have been moaning a little, because they said afterward that he had done so through all the weeks of his sickness. He could not remember that, no more than he could remember the pain. He had heard the door open softly and close, and had felt the presence of his mother. Because he had been interrupted in what he was doing, he closed his eyes and made no movement to show that he was awake. The slippered feet shuffled to a stop, and then he felt a hand creeping under the covers and coming to rest over his heart. He felt his heart beating against the pressure of the hand, and then the hand was withdrawn and he felt a kiss on his forehead. At that moment, he realized with a detached curiosity that the hand had been searching for his life.

Afterward, he had slept and he had dreamed. In the

## 8 §

dream, he was lying in his own bed and it was night, but where there had been a window before, there was now a door. Though he knew that his legs were too weak and pained to walk upon, he got out of bed anyway and found that he could stand on them easily, and without pain. He walked to the door and found that walking came easily, too. He was smiling when he opened the door, not only from the fact that he could walk but because it was so strange to find in his own room a door he did not remember ever being there.

On the other side of the door, there was another thing that he could not remember being in the house. It was a narrow stairway that mounted upward to another door. Puzzled, he climbed the steps slowly, noticing that the higher he went, the closer the air became, until it was hard to breathe. When he reached the top of the stairway, he opened the door, but this time he hesitated a little before doing so because he was wondering if he had ventured too far. When he opened the door, all there was on the other side was a little attic room, and he smiled again, because although he had never seen it, the room was familiar to him. It was a strange little room with a wooden floor and wallpaper on the walls, completely bare and with no windows.

Then he saw something that puzzled him more. When he had first looked about, he could have sworn there was no way out of the room other than the door he had used. But now there was plainly another door on the far side of the room. As he regarded it, his chest began to tighten so that he could hardly breathe, and little pricklings of terror began to course up his legs and across his back. He knew there was

## 9 §

something waiting on the other side of the door. He stood there suspended, with everything within him crying to turn around and run from the room, but crying helplessly, because he knew that he would have to open the door. And he did, crossing the room on trembling legs and reaching up to turn the knob.

He never really saw what was on the other side. Cowering like the child he was, all he knew when the door swung open was that in the darkness on the other side the thing was monstrous and black upon black, and its presence so near and so strong that without touching him it struck his senses like an invisible blow. And it was then he screamed, and the world hurled him back and forth from the attic room to his own bed and was filled with the sounds of thudding feet and the hysterical implorings of his mother and the weak flutterings of his heart and, lastly, because they were the strongest, the receding waves from the darkness beyond the door.

There was a time when he was in seminary that the dream had left him. By then he had grown into a young man with a beaked face which, with his ungainly way of walking, reminded one of a hawk flapping into flight. His childhood sickness had perhaps left a scar on his heart, but in another way it had hardened his body. He was not nearly so frail as others thought. When he was a boy and had cut or bruised himself, he would listen with a quiet amazement to the praise of his courage when he was being doctored. What they did not suspect, of course, was that he had suffered so much pain when he could feel it the worst that he would never know it again as others did. But if the sickness had taken this from him, it had given him something else, and that was a sense of the spiritual above other men, so that his awareness of the unspoken was like a living antenna.

He had never known as much happiness in his life as he had in the seminary. In the silence and solitude and coolness of stone walls and dim corridors, he had found a return of the moments of sweet mysticism he had known in his boyhood when, serving Mass in the early mornings, it would descend upon him unexpectedly and leave him at peace.

It was in seminary, too, that the dream returned. It had been his habit there to sit in a chair by the library window so that when he was studying he could look out upon the cloister and its garden of lawn and profusion of trees and flowers and, surrounding it, the open corridors where the seminarians walked in prayer and meditation.

This time, the dream had been like progression from waking to sleep. He had been lying in his cot after the lights were out, thinking idly about the chair by the library window and his pleasure in looking out upon the cloister. As he was thinking, he drifted hazily into sleep. In the dream, it was as if he were still awake. He was studying in the chair by the library window when an acrid odor pierced his nostrils and choked him so that he could hardly breathe. Mystified, he raised his head and looked about the library to see if anyone else had noticed it. But strangely, he was all alone in the room. In his surprise he sat up straight in the chair and closed his book. He looked about the room again to see if his eyes were deceiving him, but for the first time he could remember there was no one else there.

Then his turning eyes chanced to look out the window. To

## 11 §

his astonishment, the cloister and the garden had disappeared, and there was a wheatfield there. Framed in the big window, it was like a painting of a wheatfield in autumn. The colors were so brilliant that they hurt his eyes. There was a deep blue sky overhead and, as far back as he could see, an expanse of golden-crested wheat. It was altogether such an unexpected and beautiful sight that he found himself smiling in surprise. Then, suddenly, he noticed that there was something else in the wheatfield, and wondered why he had not noticed it before. He turned his gaze full upon it, and slowly he began to realize it was a man in black, or at least it resembled a man, standing in the wheatfield.

He leaned forward in his chair to see better, and made out the rude outline of a black hat and a black suit. But he could not make out the man's face. Then, unexplainably, he knew that the man was looking at him, too, and that they had seen each other before. It was then that the horror washed over him and he screamed like a child, because it was the dream of his childhood and it had taken on a shape.

## 2

When smale calder bought bandoni's garage and gas station and came to the town to live, it was a cause of some concern among the people. Not only because the only gas station in town had changed hands, but because Smale Calder was an American. Except for the lonely farm tramps who came through in planting and harvest times and stayed for a few weeks and then moved on, or the occasional curiosity seekers who chanced upon the ribbon of dirt road that connected almost invisibly to the main highway, they were not used to Americans. So isolated were they in their tiny community that they might as well have been living in another world.

Smale Calder was the first American to have set up business among them, and they did not quite know whether to be proud of it or fearful that others would come and take their town away from them. However, once they found out that Manuel Cafferata had known about it and approved, and that their credit would still be good, most of them shrugged it off with nothing more than gossip.

## 13 §

The truth of the matter was that Manuel Cafferata had not known a thing about the sale of the garage and gas station until Smale Calder had already set up shop. But this of course he could not admit to the people, since it would have been a terrible blow to his standing. When he met them on the street or when they came to the mayor's office off the middle square, he dismissed the matter with a wave of his hand and a comforting, "Don't worry about it. I have arranged the whole thing, and your credit will still be good."

Inwardly, however, he was seething with rage at the ingratitude of Bandoni, who could have done such a thing as sell his garage and gas station and actually leave town without telling him, by which he really meant without asking his permission. This when he had brought Bandoni from the railroad town to the north because he was a good mechanic, and had even gone good for a loan whereby he could go into business. The whole affair made Cafferata more convinced than ever that he had erred in bringing any of his people from the railroad town and giving them a chance to start a new life. Forgetting that this would have been impossible, he told himself that he should have peopled his town with only the young and unspoiled ones from the old country, who had nearly all worked out well, and forgotten about those who had already begun to get smart about American ways.

Joe Morelli, who sat facing him and who had his feet on Cafferata's desk, was one of these. In the railroad shops he had tried to rise too fast in the labor organization and had succeeded only in getting himself in trouble. Cafferata had taken pity on him, and brought him and his wife to the town, and in a few years Joe Morelli was sharing with him the commissions for selling the farmers' produce and grain in the county seat. Now he had a grown-up daughter, Tosca, who was something to look at even though some people said she was getting to be a tramp, and he could afford to wear a suit and smoke big cigars.

Cafferata knew that Joe Morelli was ambitious and would cut him every chance he had in ways that didn't show too much, but still he confided in him. He could not live all alone with his importance and his worries and even his deceptions, and a man had to have someone of his own kind to talk to, even if he might be an enemy.

"It makes me mad as hell," Cafferata said, slapping the desk with his meaty hand. "That ungrateful pig, after all I done for him. The only trouble with me is I got too soft a heart, to trust people who are just waiting to cut me."

The speech was meant as much for Joe Morelli as for the departed Bandoni, but Morelli listened as if he heard no meaning other than the obvious one. "You ought to know better as to trust a friend," he said, his massive face unsmiling.

"This is no matter to joke about, Morelli," said Cafferata, affecting a little hurt. "It's serious when a mayor don't know what goes on in his own town."

Joe Morelli nodded and his lidded eyes fixed on the end of the cigar he had been rolling in his mouth. "No, it's not funny," he agreed. "Do you think the people are getting tired of you?"

"They can't get tired of me," cried Cafferata. "This is my town!" Regaining his composure, he said, "And besides, they love me."

## 15 §

Morelli made placating gestures with his cigar. "I was just joking, Manuel. You know everybody loves you."

"All right, Morelli. But leave off those jokes. It's not a matter to joke about."

"Okay, okay, okay. I didn't mean nothing by it." Morelli turned his heavy eyes on Cafferata. "You going to go see this Calder fellow."

"I got to," said Cafferata, "before somebody spills the beans." He pursed his lips against the graying fringes of his mustache. "You know anything about him?"

"Oh, a little," said Morelli mysteriously.

Cafferata regarded him and decided that Morelli was lying. Still, because it was important to him, he asked, "Is he the kind of fellow who gots ideas?"

Morelli shrugged. "You never can tell about people, Manuel."

Cafferata weighed Morelli with some fatigue. "Well," he sighed. "I better get over there and let him know what goes in this town. You want to come?"

"Go ahead," said Morelli. "I'll wait for you here. When you come back, we'll go get a whisky. Settle your nerves."

He sat smoking in silence until Cafferata had picked up his black hat and puffed out the door. Then, lazily, he stood up and moved over to Cafferata's chair and sat down and put his feet back on the desk. As he watched Cafferata's portly figure cross the street and dissappear on the other side, Joe Morelli had to admire his courage if not his way of doing things. It was not an enviable job he was setting out to do, to tell a newcomer, and an American at that, who was boss in the town. If it were Morelli's job, he would have brought the message home to the newcomer in many little ways before he ever took the trouble to talk to him face to face. But this way of doing things was not in Cafferata's nature. He was a direct man and it was both his strength and his weakness.

It was like the time before the war when Cafferata had put up the big picture of Mussolini, clipped from the color section of a newspaper. Even though Morelli felt the same way Cafferata had about Mussolini, he would never have done such a rash thing as put up his picture. Because when war came, as everyone knew it probably would, the young men of the town who were going to war made an issue out of it, and Cafferata had been forced to take it down, which had not helped his standing.

As he stepped into the street, Cafferata was also thinking that it was not an enviable job he was setting out to do. If it had been an Italian he were going to see, he would have had little concern, because they would have understood each other perfectly. But an American was another animal. You could never predict him. It was the same baffling thing he had faced when he first came to America, a barrier he could not see through because he did not know or understand what had gone before.

He was so preoccupied with his thinking that when he mounted to the other sidewalk he nodded and smiled to Della Santa, the banker whom he now despised but could not get rid of because so many people were in debt to him. Peering through the grilled window of his bank, Della Santa appeared startled, and then he composed himself and nodded back. Cafferata looked at him shrewdly to see if he knew about Bandoni's sale of the garage and gas station. He guessed that the banker didn't at that, because he would have been the first to make a point of it with the people, if for no other reason than ridicule. Della Santa was a dangerous enemy, and he never missed a chance to make out that it was because of Cafferata that the town was dying.

Giometti, the butcher, was standing in the doorway of his shop with his powerful arms crossed on his chest. His apron was smeared with blood and he was dourer than usual because he had just seen Annapeta, the gypsy woman who had a hump on her back, disappearing around the corner on her daily round of trash cans. Once she had passed from sight, Giometti spit after her.

Cafferata paused in his forward progress. "Don't be so hard on the old woman, Giometti," he said. "She might put a curse on you one of these days."

"That kind of talk doesn't bother me," said Giometti, even though everyone knew that it did. He had been terrified of Annapeta from the time Joe Caneva had set his dogs to chase her out of one of his fields. The next day, Caneva's best riding horse had died in the very same field, and he had never been able to keep one alive since in that part of his farm.

Giometti's wife, a stringy little woman with a humor in her eyes that the butcher had never been able to erase, stuck her head out of the shop. She had overheard the conversation. "I've done as you said, my husband," she said with a wink at Cafferata. "I put the best meat scraps out for the gypsy woman." Giometti scowled at her, and Cafferata laughed out loud.

"If she was going to curse me, she has done it already," said Giometti. "Nobody could wish me a worse business than I already have, with the way things are going in this miserable town."

# 18 §

Cafferata took no offense at Giometti's remark. In good times or bad he was a complainer, and there wasn't much anybody could do about it. "You can always leave," said Cafferata mildly. "I can bring in somebody else anytime."

"Yeah," said Giometti. "Another American probably. What the hell you trying to do? Give the town away?"

"Don't worry about it," said Cafferata automatically. "Nothing is going to change. It's all arranged."

He was instantly not at ease, and he did not want to be drawn out into saying more, at least until he had had a chance to talk to the American. He shuffled his feet and said, "Well, I got to go on."

Giometti divined something, even if it were not the truth. "He must be something to drag you out of that office into the hot sun. Where are you going? Down to the garage to kiss his tail?"

Cafferata regarded him with eyes that had become hard and unblinking. "Sometimes you go too far, Giometti."

Giometti's dourness wavered under Cafferata's stare. "You take things too serious," he muttered.

Because the hardness was still with him, Cafferata looked away. "Well, I got to go on," he said. But before he could, a young voice hailed him from across the street. "Hey, Manuel!"

Cafferata turned in irritation. Antonio, the young man who was trotting across the street to him, was dark and good-looking, but with his hair too long and sweeping to the back of his head. "Hey, I wanta for you to do me favor," he said, in imitation of an accent.

But when he drew up in front of Cafferata and saw his

19 §

expression, he corrected himself quickly and said, "I mean it's like this, Mr. Cafferata," he said. "I need a job and I'm willing to learn the mechanic trade, and I wonder if you could put in a good word for me with the American." When Cafferata did not answer, he rattled on nervously. "What I mean is that I know Americans, you know, from when I did my service in California, and I haven't forgot all my Italian either, and I could help him out talking to some of the people here, too."

"All right, Antonio," said Cafferata. "I will put in a word for you. But you realize it's up to him if he wants you."

The young man shrugged and spread his hands in the old gesture. "Okay, that's all I want." Then he said, without any gestures, "I appreciate this, Mr. Cafferata. But tell him my name is Tony. That's the American way."

Cafferata waved the thanks aside and walked on down the street. Behind him, he heard Giometti call out to the boy. "What's the matter, punk? Your real name not good enough for you?"

"Go back to your dog sausages, butcher."

Cafferata winced but did not turn around to reprimand Antonio. Giometti had begged the insult and deserved what he got, though it would bother him little. There had been a time when Cafferata would have given the young man a tongue lashing and then taken him aside for a better kind of talk. But now it seemed not to be worth the effort. At heart, he believed him to be a good boy, but times had changed him and he had seen something of the world, and he simply did not want or fit into the old life. Still, it was curious that out of all the young ones who had come home from the war and gone away again because they had learned they could live away, Antonio should be one of the few to come back. With his long hair and smart American talk and a passion for flashy clothes, he had seemed the most rebellious of all. And yet for some reason nobody could understand he had come back and stayed, and Cafferata could not help but be touched by it.

Having tried in his own mind to find out when everything that had to do with the old life had begun to change, Cafferata had decided it was the war that had done it. It was as though the freshness and the fire that through the long years had gone into building the town and carving the fields and orchards out of the desert had flickered out.

No more the day when he would leave his office and stroll down the street in the gentle morning sun with his chest out and head high, smiling and waving hello to all his people. The widow Lucca would come running out of her bakery with a fresh roll that he must eat, and Garzoni would invite him into his new restaurant for a bite of new ravioli, just for the taste, and he could not pay for a haircut even if he wanted to. Now the widow Lucca was old and still stunned because her favorite son had been killed in Italy, of all places, and her other son was tight-fisted and did not care much for Cafferata. And Garzoni's restaurant was not new any more, but greasy and shabby, and Garzoni was bitter because his son had not stayed to help him with the business, and somehow he seemed to hold Manuel Cafferata responsible for his son's not staying.

No more the happy sight of dancing in the open street and laughter and flashing white teeth in young faces, the

## 21 §

familiar accents of Italian, and the full sounds of the accordion, and savory scents of barbecued meat and red wine, as on the summer night they had finished building the stone chapel, all working together.

Now there were only embers of the old life, and everyone was tired, like the old men with the gray mustaches sitting on the benches in front of the saloon, with their hands crossed on their canes and staring vacantly into the street. It was as if the job had been done and there was no need to think of the town any more, but only themselves and what they wanted only for themselves.

And this tiredness seemed to touch their respect for him. Remembering the years when he had not needed to demand tribute or even to think about it, Cafferata wondered exactly when it was that he had had to begin reminding people of all that he had done for them.

At least the garage was cleaner than Bandoni had ever kept it. In that, Cafferata tasted a measure of satisfaction as he stepped into the cool gloom. All the litter of junk had been cleared off the floor, and what was savable placed in neat rows against the walls. The cement floor, which already looked as if it had been scrubbed down, was being washed vigorously by a sweating Pasquale, who had also been Bandoni's handyman.

"You're working too hard, Pasquale," said Cafferata.

Pasquale grinned, showing his little tobacco-eaten teeth, but it was not a happy grin. "This is the third time today that I have cleaned this floor," he said.

"Is your boss around?"

## 22 §

Pasquale pointed to the service pit over which a pickup truck rested, and Cafferata heard the clink of metal. "Well, call him for me," he said.

"Oh, okay," said Pasquale. "Hey, boss. Someone here to see you."

The clinking continued for several seconds, and then stopped, as if the man were methodically finishing one task before going on to another. There was a sound of movement, and then Cafferata saw a broad back and a gray shirt emerging out of the pit.

From the moment that their eyes met, Cafferata knew two things: that he had nothing to fear from this man Smale Calder and, also, that he had never met anyone quite like him.

It had nothing particular to do with the way he looked, because he was a colorless man. He was big, not tall, but with a massive breadth of chest and, curiously for one who worked with his hands, almost clumsy in his movements. The skin of his face was thick and sallow, and his short, lank hair sat on his head like a cap. And strangely, too, because his face was not gentle, there was hidden somewhere in his pale blue eyes what could almost be called gentleness.

"Yeah?" he said, walking unhurriedly to where Manuel Cafferata stood.

For an instant Cafferata was taken aback by the impersonality of it all. Though he had never seen Calder before, he had assumed that the man would at least know who he was, as everyone else did in the town.

"My name is Manuel Cafferata," he said finally.

"Pleased to meet you," said Calder slowly, in a tone that

showed the name meant nothing to him. "I'd shake your hand but I got grease on mine."

"Think nothing of it. These hands have known grease before."

Calder regarded him with no change of expression. "Is that so?" he said simply, but did not extend his hand.

Cafferata was becoming a little irritated, especially since Pasquale had stopped scrubbing and was watching the scene, with his mouth open as usual. "I'm the mayor of this town," he said firmly. "I guess Bandoni told you that."

"No, he didn't. But then, I didn't ask him."

Cafferata was almost at a loss what to say, but he knew he had to say something, and quickly and in the right way. "I want you to know I approved this sale so that you could come here," he said, sensing that he was on safe ground because of Bandoni's silence, ungrateful though it was.

"Well, I'm much obliged."

"And I guess you know the arrangement we have here about credit for our people until they can pay."

After a moment, Calder said, "I've been in little towns before. That's the way I always operate."

At least he had not met the question head on, and for that Cafferata was thankful, though he knew that Calder had not avoided it purposely. Cafferata cleared his throat. "There's another thing. We try to help out our young boys whenever we can, and there's a boy, Tony Bianchi by name, who wants to talk to you about a job. He's a good boy. A little wild, but a good boy."

Calder scratched the back of his head. "I don't rightly know whether I need him. But maybe we can work something out. You tell him to come around, and I'll think about it a while."

"I will. And anything I can do to help your business, you let me know."

"Much obliged. But I don't think I'll be needing any favors."

"You never can tell," said Cafferata, refusing to be rebuffed. "And I'm the man that can help you out."

When Calder said nothing but began to regard him with faint puzzlement, Cafferata bit nervously at the fringes of his mustache. "You know, there's a story they tell about me," he said. "Before the war, when I was building this town, I used to arrange to bring people here from the old country. I made the arrangements with the immigration, and got passage money for them and jobs so they could pay it back, and loaned them money when they needed it, and took care of their business with the Americans, and talked to them about their troubles, and just about everything else you could think of. So it come that once when one of them was taking his citizenship papers in the city, they asked him who was president of the United States, and he said, 'Manuel Cafferata.'"

Smale Calder grinned. "Well, that's a pretty good story. But I'm wondering whether it's the people who tell the story, or you."

As he walked back up the street toward his office, Cafferata thought that he would like a whisky after all. Not that the meeting had come off bad, or good, either. He had been uncomfortable in Smale Calder's presence, and he was relieved to be away from him. There was something about

Calder that he could not fathom, a privacy that he could not pass through. It was as though he had met a man who lived all alone in the world and did not even need other men or anything they could give him.

But at the same time Cafferata knew that he would not have to have much to do with Calder and, more importantly, nothing to fear from him. He was plainly the kind of person who would bother no one.

# 3

FATHER SAVIO LAZZARONI TUCKED IN a frayed end of the vestment and pushed the drawer shut. He was still clad in the flowing alb, and he plucked in agitation at the cincture that bound it tightly around his waist. Without turning to face Amado, the young man who had served at Mass for him, he asked casually, "What kind of person is he?"

The young man was sitting in the sacristy's lone chair, and he had been watching the unvesting in quiet absorption. "I don't know him myself, Father," he said as if he had been thinking of something else. "All I know is what I've heard, but mostly what Tony Bianchi has told me about him. He works at the garage now."

Father Savio was pulling the wide skirt of the alb over his head. "I wouldn't put much faith in what that boy has to say," he muttered through the folds of cloth.

"I didn't hear you, Father."

Father Savio laid the alb on the table and smoothed his

hair back from his hawked face. "I said I don't think much of Tony Bianchi."

Amado's sensitive brown eyes showed a pang of guilt. "Well, he's not exactly my friend, Father," he said lamely. "But we grew up together, you know."

"I didn't ask whether he was your friend, Amado," Father Savio reminded him. "Your friends are your own business. But it's a shame some of your goodness didn't wash off on him."

"Tony's not all bad," Amado began, and then realized what he had affirmed about himself. His face flushed and the embarrassment in his eyes was painful. "I mean, I'm not so good either . . ." he faltered.

It occurred to Father Savio that he had never seen eyes that were so revealing as Amado's. Then, at the same time, he knew that the reason the thought had occurred to him was what had happened the day before. He turned away in momentary confusion of his own and pretended to take pains with hanging the alb in the closet. "That's enough of Tony Bianchi," he said with dismissal.

Amado felt that he had to explain. "He's not all bad, Father. It's just that he changed a lot when he went away. But when we were growing up, he was always good to me. And you know, not all the boys were."

"That might be one thing in his favor," said Father Savio. "But I would say he has made up for his goodness since then. You don't have to defend Tony Bianchi to me. I've judged him for myself. Anyone who has so little respect as to pass his church at night carrying on with a girl like

Tosca Morelli—and I am not revealing anything that is not common gossip in this town—is not a good boy."

Amado's face had turned deep red, and Father Savio was suddenly impatient with him for it. "That's quite enough of Tony Bianchi's character," he said firmly. Then, realizing that he had almost closed the door on what he had wanted to learn in the first place, he said, "Now, where were we? Oh yes, the man at the garage."

"Smale Calder, his name is," said Amado. He paused, collecting his thoughts. "Tony—I mean, people say . . ."

"Oh, go ahead," said Father Savio.

Amado sighed. "Well, Tony says he doesn't talk much, or hardly at all for that matter, except to tell him what to do. Other than that, he acts like he doesn't even know Tony is there."

"He doesn't sound like a pleasant working companion."

"I don't know," said Amado evasively. "Tony says the man isn't at all bad to him." He paused, as if remembering something. "Nor good either." He was detached for a moment. "Now, that's a funny thing to say."

Father Savio rubbed his hands together. Though he had not thought the sacristy was cold, he had felt a chill. "Yes, it is a funny thing to say." Amado was regarding him wonderingly, and Father Savio said, "What does this man do outside of his work?"

Amado shrugged. "He lives in the little house off the garage, and does his own cooking. He doesn't do much of anything else, I guess, except that he takes walks at night."

"At night!" Father Savio exclaimed.

"Not really at night," Amado said hastily. "At sundown.

29

I've heard it from others. He walks out into the desert at the end of the day."

Father Savio would have liked to know much more, but he did not want to risk seeming too curious. "Well, there's nothing wrong with that," he said lightly, and rubbed his hands together again. "Would you like to have breakfast with me in the house? Your mother must have it ready by now."

"I'd better not. I'll be late to work. I can get a cup of coffee at the store."

They went out the sacristy door into the sunlight. The morning was clear, and reflecting against the stone wall of the chapel, the sun was already beginning to be hot.

"I'm sorry I held you so long," said Father Savio. "But we don't often get a chance to talk these days. Are you still praying for your vocation?"

"Yes," said Amado with what seemed to Father Savio a little discomfort. "But I can't seem to make up my mind it's the right thing to do." He stopped in shocked protest of his own words. "I mean that it's the right thing for me to do, until God has told me that I should." Still quailing at the terrible flare that was even now fading too slowly in Father Savio's face, he said abjectly, "I can't seem to make my words say what I mean."

With an effort, Father Savio said, "Well, there's nothing wrong with that. It shows an honest heart."

But as he hurried away, almost in a trot because he was late to work, Amado wondered what Father Savio really thought. The priest was not one to forget such slips easily, and he had pointed out to Amado before that the clues to truth were hidden in the unpronounced. And that was the trouble. Amado had gotten so used to conceiving of Father Savio as one who spoke in such attractive terms of despair with the world, but about nobody in particular, that the morning's experience had been a puzzling one. He could not remember when he had seen the priest so curious as he was about the man at the garage.

Father Savio had not needed Amado's instruction in the matter. He knew what Smale Calder's name was, and he had known it all along. From the first moment he had heard the name, and that there was a man in town who was an American, he had sensed a vague uneasiness. There was no particular reason for it, because, after all, Father Savio was not of the town, either. He had been reared in the city among the Americans, as the immigrants put it, and they were no novelty to him.

So, wondering at his uneasiness, he decided that it had somehow sprung from the way in which the townspeople imparted the information to him. Though there had been nothing obvious in their simple telling of the news, Father Savio knew that there were omens even in innocence. And the innocent were the last to be aware of them.

His curiosity had moved him the day before to take a walk downtown to the vicinity of the garage. He had dropped into the store where Amado worked, and had surprised him talking with Tosca Morelli. Amado had been embarrassed by it, but being preoccupied at the time, Father Savio did not remember until later. Tosca Morelli had smiled a greeting with her tiny white teeth and black eyes that always seemed to be hiding an unpretty secret, and had made an unhurried

31 §

exit. Father Savio had busied himself with looking over the cluttered array of things on the shelves near the window.

When Amado went into the back room on some duty, Father Savio from time to time glanced through the dusty window at the garage, which was almost directly across the street. It was morning, and Pasquale was busy in the dark doorway of the garage, sweeping out the dirt with unexpected vigor.

Then he had stopped sweeping, as if listening to someone speaking, and Smale Calder's figure had suddenly emerged from the gloom. Father Savio had turned his head away so quickly that he had not had time to see more than a blurred image of the man. For a long moment Father Savio kept all his concentration focused on the shelves, because he could sense that Smale Calder was looking at him. When he could bear it no longer, he turned with exaggerated calmness to gaze out the window again. He had been right. Smale Calder was standing against the darkness of the garage, and the bright morning sun was full upon him, so that Father Savio could see his face clearly. Their eyes met and locked, and then Father Savio heard the sounds of Amado's coming and again he turned away too quickly, though he had tried not to.

Later, he told himself that he was making too much of the thing, that, after all, Calder was just a man like any other man. But when he did so, the memory of the shapeless figure and the expressionless eyes in the sallow face returned to him with a wave of revulsion. There was a quality about the man that was different. Of that much Father Savio was certain. And though the whole of his being rebelled against finding out what it was, he knew that he would have to, with the same helplessness of his childhood dream and the attic door.

The conversation with Amado had done nothing to dispel what he felt, but rather had sharpened it so that he could think of nothing else at his breakfast after Mass.

The hovering presence of Mrs. Ricco, Amado's ponderous mother, who cooked the priest's meals and kept house for him in the daytime, was annoying to the point that he could hardly bear her. It was one of her days for talking, and about Amado, and he was not interested in hearing about Amado at this moment.

"He's a good boy, Father. I know he will make a good priest. The best there is," she said, and added with a generous smile, "Except for you, of course."

"He hasn't made up his mind about the priesthood, you know," said Father Savio through a mouthful of food.

She shrugged it aside. "That's just talk. This idea he's got in his mind to be a singer is just talk. It came from his father." She made the sign of the cross. "He used to tell Amado that if a man had music, the world would open its arms to him. He would tell Amado the story of a thing that happened when he came to America. He got off the train in the big city, and there was no one there to meet him. He tried to ask the people, but they couldn't understand him. He waited and waited, and nobody came. So, in his sadness, he went down the tracks to a bench where he could be alone, and there he played his accordion and he sang. The people gathered around to hear him, and they wouldn't let him stop. Afterward, a couple of the men took him into town to the Italian hotel, and there he found out where he was supposed to go." She made a gesture as if to brush away a tear. "He had a way of saying things that would make your head turn. He said that when God breathed a man's life into him, He breathed a little longer to make a singer." Her expression changed deliberately. "But he was a weak man with the women," she said darkly. "The things I could tell you."

Despite himself, the story caught Father Savio's attention, but in a troubled way, because there was a hidden truth in it he could not quite understand. And so, finally, it angered him even more. "Is Amado much like his father?" he asked with undisguised malice.

She looked stunned for an instant. "No!" she protested, jabbing at her mountainous bosom punishingly. "He is not like his father. He is like me."

"I saw him talking with Tosca Morelli the other day," said Father Savio.

The transfiguring of her face was a thing to behold. The smile of piety that she wore in his presence vanished as suddenly as if she had been slapped, and he felt the full force of her being. "If Amado was talking to her, it was because he is polite," she said, waving her broad finger almost in his face. "He don't have nothing to do with tramps like that."

Father Savio regretted what he had said. Not because he had succeeded in making her reveal herself, but because of the furious strength he had unleashed. He did his best to pacify her. For the most part, he succeeded, but even when he left the parish house Mrs. Ricco's eyes were still showing fire. He could feel no sympathy for her. As for Amado, it was a different thing. He would be facing a very uncomfortable evening with his mother, and probably out of complete innocence. For that, Father Savio knew a pang of guilt.

So he had stopped at what went for a bank in the town and gone over the parish accounts with Della Santa, and had even dropped in to say hello and parry uncomfortably a while with Manuel Cafferata and the silent Joe Morelli. And now he crossed the street to talk child's talk with little Luigi, who had a box of matches and was burning ants in the gutter.

It was the closest that Father Savio had yet approached the garage. Throughout his tour, he had been circling around it, drawn nearer to the dark doorway, beyond which he could see nothing but from time to time could hear sounds of activity. Within the thin pretense of his actions, he had felt ridiculous more than once. It was not the right way to go about it, and he realized this painfully. But once he had started, there seemed to be no other course but to follow it through.

Looking down upon the mass of tight blond curls that was the top of little Luigi's head, he said vaguely, "How is life treating you, my young man?"

Squatting on his thin haunches, Luigi was tormenting a big red ant, turning him this way and that with the nearness of the flame. "Nobody treats me good and I'm not a young man. I'm a little boy," said Luigi, touching the match to the ant.

Father Savio regarded the shriveled body of the ant, fascinated by the swiftness with which it had died. The

## 35 §

ground around Luigi's bare feet was littered with burned matches and dead, blackened ants. It was curiously like a graveyard. "That's not a very nice way to speak to your priest," said Father Savio.

Luigi did not answer. He had learned very early that silence was the best answer to questions of this sort, or most questions, for that matter. He had come upon the lesson by accident, having been shocked into a real muteness by the senseless murder of his mother and the suicide of his father, so that he could not have answered those questions if he had wanted to. Later, when he had been thrust upon the town's care and had moved about, living first with one family and then another, he had used the dumbness to his advantage. It was the only way he could avoid the probing of those who wanted to know what went on in other people's houses.

When it became obvious that he was no longer a mute, he had fallen back on unexplained silences and blank stares. It had been necessary, especially now that he had chosen to live awhile with Annapeta in her tin-can shack outside of town. It had been successful, too, since nobody knew any more about Annapeta than they did before.

Father Savio leaned over to watch more closely. Luigi had struck another match and was preoccupied in herding three ants into a group. Two of them complied, but the third was bent on escape. Luigi touched the match to the two, but before he could reach the third the flame scorched his fingers and he had to drop it. In a gesture of fury, he squashed the third one with his finger. Though the ant was broken, he was still alive. Unhurriedly, Luigi struck a match and held it above the ant, but not near enough to kill him at once. The child was a perfectionist in this kind of killing, and the ant died slowly.

There was the crunch of footsteps on dirt, and Father Savio looked up to see the hulking shape and blazing eyes of Smale Calder. The matches were jerked from Luigi's grasp, and the boy was knocked onto his back by one cuff of a big hand. Father Savio leaped back in terror, but Smale Calder was not paying any attention to him. He was busy stamping out the charred evidence of Luigi's work.

When he was done, he stood over Luigi. "If I ever catch you burning ants again, I'll give you a beating you're not likely to forget."

There were no tears in Luigi's eyes. Still sitting in the dirt, his mouth was open in surprise. After a moment, he scrambled to his feet and walked away, looking back once in sullen defiance.

Smale Calder turned to face Father Savio. He was shaking with anger. "I don't know what kind of a man you are to stand by and watch what you were watching."

Father Savio gasped in protest. "Now, just a minute here."

"You ought to be ashamed of yourself."

"Mr. Calder," said Father Savio, his voice rising. "You're talking to a priest."

He was aware that Pasquale had come out of the garage and was listening in shocked attention. And there were probably others who were listening from the street behind him. He made a wrenching effort to recapture his self-control. "I'm not going to argue with you about the actions of a demented boy. Whether you're aware of it or not, that boy saw his father kill his mother and then himself. He hasn't been the same since, and everybody in this town knows it and excuses it."

"That's his excuse," said Calder. "Now, what's yours?"

It was said with such contempt that for an instant Father Savio could not comprehend the full meaning of what he had heard. When he did, the color drained from his face and he was struck speechless. It would not have made any difference anyway, because by then Smale Calder had turned his back on him and was walking away, with only a sideward glance at the place in the street where the dirt was still stained with ashes.

# 4

"Right down there," said Tony. "Down in those rocks." When Smale Calder paused, debating whether to leave the truck in the middle of the narrow dirt road or pull it off to the side, Tony said, "You can leave it right here. There's not a dozen cars a year come up this road."

Smale Calder pulled the truck to the side of the road, smashing sagebrush under the heavy tires. "Just in case," he said, and they got out of the truck and started down the hillside. Tony went ahead, picking his way through the brush. He had taken off his shirt at the machinery dump early that morning, and his shoulders were burned red. "I hope we can get a drink," said Tony. "This spring dries up a little later, but there's usually enough running now to get a drink."

"I could use one for sure," said Smale Calder. He was coming down the hillside with more difficulty, and there was already a considerable space between them. He had been sweating, and his shirt was stuck to his back.

There was a jumble of boulders at the bottom of the

ravine, and Tony leaped lightly from one to another until he came to a flat rock that sloped down to the spring. Lying prone, he leaned over to drink at the trickle of water. Behind him, Smale Calder reached the bottom of the ravine and was moving laboriously through the boulders.

The rattlesnake must have been sleeping in the sun, because it did not seem to come awake until Tony sat up to catch his breath from drinking. If it had been even a foot farther away, Tony would have jumped. But it was on a ledge almost even with his face, and so near that when the whirring started, he could not have moved if he had wanted to. He heard the sound and identified it, and then the thinking part of him turned off and he was transfixed. The only movement he made, and that was so incredibly slow that it was like no movement at all, was to incline his head slightly for a better view of the snake. He saw the spade head pulled back in a coil like a buttonhook, the opaque and senseless eyes, and the flickering tongue that was wet and black, and thought, *He is going to bite me on the mouth.*

When Smale Calder spoke, it seemed that it was from a long way off. "Don't move, kid. Don't move a muscle or you're dead." Then a little later, in the same flat, unhurried command, "If you can't stand to look, close your eyes. But don't move!"

Tony closed his eyes, but it did not make much difference in what he was seeing. The whirring sound, rising and falling in indecision, was there to remind him of what was coiled on the ledge in front of his face. The numbness that had encased him was beginning to creep away. Behind him, he heard Smale Calder's movements and wondered when the crash of the rock would come. *He had better not miss,* thought Tony, *but even if he does, I am going to jump.* He heard Smale Calder talking. It was in a voice he had never heard before. It reminded him of a child's tuneless singing. Then, unexplainably, Tony knew that Smale Calder was not going to kill the snake. The knowledge made the perspiration start cold from his forehead and run down into the corners of his mouth.

He felt Smale Calder's pantlegs brush his bare shoulders and smelled his sweaty presence. Then the dry sound of the snake's whirring faded to an occasional rustle and died out. Calder's pantlegs brushed him again and he heard the sound of retreating footsteps, and he realized with a returning wave of terror that the man had gone away. Because he could not have contained himself any more, with nerves running like fire through his body, he tensed to jump. Then Calder's voice came to him from a distance. "It's all right now. But don't get close to me. Take the truck and go on home. I'll be along later."

Tony opened his eyes. The ledge in front of him was bare. His senses reeled and he almost fainted. He shook his head to settle the spinning world about him. When his strength returned, he stood up to look for Smale Calder. The man was mounting the hillside, but in a direction away from the truck. He had his arms crossed in front of him, and he was holding something. Tony did not look at him any more, but climbed the hillside on unsteady legs.

Before he got into the truck, he looked back. Smale Calder was walking toward the road again, but slowly, and with his head bent to what he was holding in his arms. It occurred to Tony that one of Calder's arms was very thick, and that there was something dangling from it. Then he admitted to himself that Smale Calder was holding the rattlesnake, and that it was alive. Tony got into the truck and started to drive away, hoping his sickness would hold off until he had passed over the concealing rim of the hill.

Because Manuel Cafferata and Joe Morelli had been to the county seat together and returned later than their usual hour, Tony repeated the story again. He did not mind, since it was easier the second time. Besides, some of the old men on the benches outside had heard about what happened and came into the saloon to listen, too. When he finished, Piumbo, the bartender, poured him a new shot glass of whisky. Tony's hand still trembled a little when he reached for it.

"To come that close to dying is no joke," said Piumbo. "If he had gotten you in the face, you wouldn't be here now."

Except for a sympathetic whistle, Manuel Cafferata had been silent when the story was being told. "Well, you got to thank this fellow Calder for saving your life."

"You don't have to tell me that," said Tony. With the whisky, the blood had returned to his face, except for a pallor that still lingered around his mouth.

The butcher, Giometti, was at the bar, too. "To pick up a goddamned rattlesnake in your bare hands." He scowled and shuddered at the same time. "I would have to see it to believe it."

"You calling me a liar, Giometti?"

"Settle down, punk. I'm not talking about you. I'm talking about this guy Calder."

"It's a pretty good trick," said Joe Morelli.

Tony shrugged. "I don't know whether it's a trick or not. I just know he did it, even if Giometti believes me or not."

"All right, all right," said Manuel Cafferata. "Leave off the fighting for a while." He was still a little uncomprehending because he had not really believed the part about Smale Calder picking up the snake in his hands. "Do you mean to say he brought that thing back into town?"

"I can't say that for sure. All I know, he was still holding it when I saw him the last time."

"But he wouldn't dare to bring a rattlesnake into town," said Cafferata.

"I don't see why not," said Joe Morelli dryly. "It won't be lonesome with some people I know in this town."

"Don't make jokes about that kind of thing, Morelli," said Cafferata. "It just don't seem right, to bring a snake into town."

"He has probably killed it by now," said Tony. Then, not believing this, he said, "Or maybe he turned the snake loose."

Pasquale had been standing at the end of the bar, out of the circle of conversation. "Oh, he will bring him back all right," he said.

Manuel Cafferata turned, taking notice of Pasquale. "What makes you say that?"

Pasquale grinned and showed his stained teeth. "Because Calder has got another one that maybe needs company. He keeps him in a big box in the house. I saw the thing one day when I sneaked in to look for some wine, but I didn't find any."

## 43 §

"You're crazy, Pasquale," said Cafferata.

"No, I am not crazy. After he scared me, I went back to look at him again. He's the meanest rattlesnake I ever saw. And the biggest, too." Pasquale calculated Giometti's height. "He's easy bigger than Giometti."

It was dusk when Smale Calder reached the outskirts of the town, and the dusk was warm with the heat that was still in the earth. Far to the west, there was a glow of fire on the horizon as of a halo receding from the night's advance. In the town, the windows of the houses were already framed with light.

He had loitered along the way until the time the street would be deserted, and now he quickened his pace so as to reach the garage before meeting anyone. A figure detached itself from the shadows on the side of the street, but it was only old Annapeta on her way home to her shack, with a gunny sack of pickings from trash cans slung over her shoulder. Smale Calder passed her without a glance. Unknown to him, she stopped after he had gone by, as if her thoughts had been interrupted, and arched her wrinkled neck out of the black shawl to stare after him.

The garage was open and unlighted, and Calder guessed that Tony and Pasquale had already left for the day. The kid was probably having a drink in the saloon. God knew he needed it after what had happened to him. Remembering Tony's white face and the cold sweat beading on his brow, Smale Calder could not help wondering how it must feel to be so afraid.

Because it was a failing with him to stumble easily, he

picked his way with care through the garage and the yard that lay between it and the house. The screen door squeaked a little, so he let it close behind him gently. He was prepared for what would happen when he stepped into the kitchen and turned on the light.

The snake had been lying with one loose coil around his arm, resting mostly against his stomach. When the furious buzzing began in the long box under the table, the snake tightened in alarm. "Now, just take it easy," Smale Calder said, and at the same time put his hand over the snake's head and stroked the side of it with his thumb. "Don't mind that overgrown brute and all his noise. He's more bluff than bother."

Yet, when he reached for the latch string on the top of the box, the rattling inside grew even more furious. There was a sudden thump against the panel, so hard that he could feel it through the wood. Calder had been expecting that, too. With a cluck of annoyance, he said, "So it's going to be that way. Sometimes I wonder why in the hell I keep you. You got such a nasty temper."

The snake he was holding was quiet again, and Calder looked around the kitchen and finally decided to put him in the sink. He was not a big snake, and he found his way to a corner of the sink and coiled there comfortably. He was gray, and against the white surface, the mottled brown blotches on his back took on a clear pattern. Smale Calder paused to admire him.

The snake seemed content to stay where he was for the moment, and Calder turned his back on him and went into the pantry that stood off the kitchen. There was a cage there with field mice inside, and he reached in and grasped one of the squirming bodies in his big hand. He went back to the long box in the kitchen and held the mouse near the latch string until the buzzing inside subsided and grew quiet.

When Calder slid back the panel, the light shone into the box. He was a huge snake, with coils the size of a man's arm lying one upon the other and a great spade head resting on the mass. The light glistened against the moist black of his flickering tongue, and the yellow bars in his eyes showed clearly. He was a golden brown in color, and there was gold, too, in the vivid chain of diamonds that ran along his back. Looking at him, Calder said, "The only good a man can say for you is that you're a beautiful damn thing." He dropped the mouse inside the box and closed the panel.

For a time there was a scurrying of little feet on the sand in the box. There was a thud like a muffled blow and then a squeal, coming almost together. Smale Calder winced. He waited until he could hear no sound of movement in the box, and then he picked up the snake in the sink and slid back the panel again.

The diamondback had retrieved the mouse and he was beginning to swallow it. He paid no attention when Calder let the snake in his hands slip into the box. The new arrival seemed also to be oblivious of the diamondback and what he was doing. He raised his head once to survey his surroundings, and then crawled into a corner. "Well, I hope the brute learns some good manners from you," said Calder, and slid the panel closed.

Later, when he went back to the garage to pull shut the big sliding door, he saw two men coming out of the saloon.

Against the light, he made out Manuel Cafferata's portly figure. He did not recognize the man with him. Cafferata was excited about something. He was gesturing with his hands and talking. Calder could not hear what he was saying. The man with him was puffing on a cigar, and he seemed to be unperturbed. Standing in the darkness, Calder watched them as they went up the street to the dingy restaurant. He wondered idly what had made Manuel Cafferata so concerned. But then, Cafferata seemed the kind of man who was always concerned. Smale Calder yawned and stretched and pulled the big door mostly shut. This time, when he made his way through the garage, he could afford to be less careful.

## 5

THE PIT WAS CIRCULAR, AND THEY had dug it in the yard behind the garage. There was a young cottonwood tree nearby, and its shade fell partially over the hole. "You got to have shade," Smale Calder said, "A snake can't take the sun like most people think."

It had taken Tony a while to realize that the house Calder meant when they started to dig was a house for his snakes. Calder had been amused at his look of incredulity, but he said nothing. He heaved a last shovelful of dirt out of the pit and patted the ground smooth. Tony leaned on his shovel and let the first ripplings of the afternoon breeze cool him. His eyes were still bloodshot and his face was puffed from the whisky he had drunk the night before, but he was feeling better.

"Now we put the rocks around," said Calder. From the pile he had gathered in the desert, he chose two rocks for a base and then a huge slab, and placed them in the exact center of the pit. "This will be for the brute," he said. "He'll be king regardless."

## 48 §

They placed the other rocks in a semicircle on the far side of the pit, so that they would be in the afternoon shade. Calder stacked them to his own taste, smiling occasionally to himself when he made a good fit. Tony watched him quietly, seeing the pleasure that the man was taking in his work. Ever since they had started to dig the pit that morning, Calder acted altogether differently from the way he did in the garage. He reminded Tony of a child absorbed in a task of secret peace.

When he finished, the rocks were a labyrinth of caves and crevices that opened upon each other in twists and turns, so that one could trace a dozen routes that a snake might take upon entering and leaving. Afterward, they set up iron stakes along the inside rim of the pit and strung a double thickness of chickenwire so fine that it was like a screen. Then, a foot farther back, they strung still another enclosure of the chickenwire, so that there was an intervening space between. The last thing they placed in the pit was a flat rock with a natural hollow in it, which Calder filled with water.

"Is that a bathtub?" Tony asked.

Calder looked at him sharply and saw that he was serious. "No. Snakes got to drink water too, you know."

"I didn't know. I never thought about it before."

"That's that," said Calder when the flat rock was settled. "Now we show our snakes their new house."

Tony stepped back. "If you don't mind, Mr. Calder, I would just as soon not."

Smale Calder grinned. "I didn't mean you, kid. Fact is, you better stand over by the garage door so's you'll be out of sight and smell. It don't usually make a difference, but with the brute, you never can tell."

## 49 §

Tony retreated to the garage door and found Pasquale there. "You're supposed to stay out."

"You don't have to say it. I heard him. Anyway, you think I'm crazy enough to go closer?"

Smale Calder disappeared inside the little house, and Tony and Pasquale fell silent. They could hear no sound, and after a while Tony began to get nervous.

"You think something's happened to him?"

Pasquale shrugged. "I don't know that."

"Maybe we ought to go in."

Pasquale grinned feebly. "No, I am not going in."

"But what if he got bit by the brute?"

"One getting bit is better as two getting bit," said Pasquale. "I am not going in."

"I wonder if I ought to call him."

"You better not. You could make trouble."

"Damn it, I don't know what to do."

"Then don't do nothing, I tell you," said Pasquale.

"For Christ's sake, shut up." Tony looked around for something with which to arm himself so that he could go into the house.

Pasquale hissed and Tony looked around to see the screen door opening softly. Smale Calder came deliberately down the single step and walked across the yard. He was holding a snake in his hands. But the snake was not fighting. He was cradled so limply that his tail was even hanging loose, as if he were dead. When he realized that it was the rattlesnake that had almost bitten him the day before, Tony leaned weakly against the door. At his side, he heard Pasquale breathing noisily through his teeth.

Smale Calder stepped down carefully into the pit and

crossed to the labyrinth. He got down on his knees and set the snake on the ground so that his head was pointed toward one of the openings in the rocks. The snake did not enter immediately but raised his head to look about. The black fork of his tongue was spread and quivering. He was between Calder's knees, and when he waved his head, his tongue seemed to be touching the man's bare forearms. The snake regarded the rocks with the same measured deliberation, and then he flattened out and went into the opening in a cautious, gliding movement. When his rattle had disappeared, Smale Calder got to his feet and absently brushed the dirt from his hands. His face was set in a mask, and his lower lip protruded slightly, as when Tony had seen him absorbed over some piece of work in the garage. He did not even look about, but stepped out of the pit, leaving the gate open, and crossed the yard to the house.

"Santa Maria!" said Pasquale.

Tony sighed and wondered if he had even been breathing. "Did you ever see such a thing?"

"No," said Pasquale. "And I don't want to see it no more."

"You better stay. The brute is coming next. There could be trouble."

Pasquale had not exaggerated when in Piumbo's saloon he said that it was the biggest rattlesnake he had ever seen. It was as though Smale Calder were holding a mountain of coils in his two arms. They were of a color Tony had never seen—so gold that they gleamed in the slanting rays of the sun. As big as Calder was, he was somehow diminished in size by the snake, and Tony could sense that the man knew it. Calder moved with exaggerated slowness across the yard. One of his hands was resting lightly but warily at the base of the snake's great head.

Neither Tony nor Pasquale had noticed the boy entering the garage. The first that Tony knew of what was happening was when he felt someone brush his leg, and he glanced down to see Luigi's blond curls. By then the boy was already past him. Squealing with delight, Luigi ran to the wire fence that surrounded the pit and began jumping up and down in excitement.

Calder had been in the act of setting the brute snake in front of the big cave he had fashioned for him. At the commotion, the relaxed coils instantly became a boiling mass of movement. Calder looked back at the boy once in surprise and rage. His arms waving helplessly in search of a weapon, Tony leaped forward to help Calder.

"Get back!" Calder shouted. "Keep away from me!" His hand was clamped like a vise on the snake's neck, and the other was searching to grip the squirming coils. For a moment it seemed that he would not succeed and that the brute snake would twist himself free. Then Calder found a hold and the snake was secure. Dropping swiftly down on one knee, he shoved the snake's head into the confines of the rock cave. Letting loose his hold, he jumped back and lumbered out of the pit. The brute snake recovered in one lightning movement and was gliding furiously after him when Calder pushed the gate shut. As though he were unaware of the wire mesh that separated him from the man, the snake whipped into a coil and struck. The gaping mouth hit with such force that the unhinged fangs were entangled in the mesh and the snake was caught. He twisted painfully to free himself. Calder cried out and reached to open the gate.

Tony would have been too late to stop Calder, but the snake shook himself free of the wire. Calder pushed the gate shut. The brute snake coiled again but did not strike. He lay back in his coil, and his whirring tail was an angry blur. He had cut his nose against the wire, and a thin line of blood began to show.

Calder latched the gate and leaned against it, breathing hard. After a while he looked at Luigi. The boy was standing at the fence with his mouth open. He was gazing in adoration at Smale Calder.

"Damn you!" Calder said. He moved as if to hit the boy, but Luigi moved out of range and continued to regard him adoringly. "Oh, for Christ's sake," said Calder and turned his back on him.

Pasquale was still hiding in the doorway to the garage. He was so pale that the roots of his whiskers stood out black. Tony walked to Calder's side and looked apprehensively into the pit at the big snake. "That was too close."

"It's not the brute's fault," said Calder. "Look at him now. He's hurt good."

"That thing scares me to death," Tony said.

"He'll gentle down some after a while. But for now, he's mad and he's hurt, and I better make my peace with him or he'll never let me into that pit." He looked around at them absently. "You can clean up inside and go on home," he said to Tony. "Don't come out here in the yard any more. And will you get rid of that kid!"

Because he would be of little help that day, Tony sent

Pasquale out at the same time as Luigi. Then he gathered the tools and swept the floor. Before he closed up the garage, however, he could not resist peeking through the back door. Smale Calder was kneeling by the fence, talking to the brute snake in the same tuneless child's voice that Tony had heard in the desert. The snake was still coiled, but his head was up and looking at Calder, and his tongue was flickering. It was curiously like two people talking together.

Tony walked quietly back across the garage and pulled shut the big door. He glanced once at Piumbo's saloon and decided that he would rather take a walk. He thought about walking alone, but he was too disturbed for that. He decided to go by Tosca Morelli's house and see if she wanted to come with him. When one wanted to think over things, walking with Tosca was, for a while at least, like being alone.

As they sauntered past houses and people on their way out of town, Tosca Morelli was playing a private game. "I don't like them. I don't like him. I like them a little. You know," she said, "I don't like very many people in this town."

Tony had been caught up in his own thoughts. "What?"

"I said I don't like anybody in this town." Tosca kicked at him. "Why do you take me for a walk if you don't listen to anything I say?"

"You didn't have to come with me."

"Would you like it if I didn't?"

Tony returned her taunt with a sidling glance of his own, letting his eyes play purposely over the firm pointings of her breasts. "No, I guess not."

"Then be nice to me."

"All right, what did you say?"

"I said I don't like very many people in this town. I want to go away."

"Then why don't you go away?"

"Why don't you marry me and take me away?"

Tony shrugged. "If I had any money, I'd buy me a car."

Tosca bared her small even teeth. "I think I'll bite you right here in the street."

"You better not," said Tony seriously. "We're in front of the church."

"I don't care," said Tosca, tossing her black hair. "He can't say anything about me he hasn't said already." She thought a moment. "I like him least of all. Do you like him?"

"I don't know. I haven't thought about it. I don't think so, though."

"Why not?"

"Because he's always looking inside of me, and that's none of his business," blurted Tony. He stopped himself. "We shouldn't talk like this about a priest."

"Why not? He's human, too."

Amado Ricco stepped unexpectedly through the white gate in front of the priest's house. Because of the bushes that hid the street, he had not seen them. When he did, he was embarrassed.

"Hi, Amado," Tony said.

Amado said hello but studiously avoided Tosca with his eyes. She did not resent it, but, instead, regarded him with a little smile on her lips. Tony sensed something, but concealed his amusement. "You know Tosca, don't you?"

"Yes," said Amado. "Well, of course I do."

## 55 §

"You didn't say hello to her."

"Yes, I did," said Amado helplessly.

Tony grinned. "I'm sorry, Amado. I was just teasing."

Amado forced a laugh. He wished that he had seen them coming before he left the garden. At the same time, he did not want to leave them. He thought he felt eyes peering from the house behind him, but he could not be sure whether they were his mother's or the priest's.

"How is the Father?" Tony asked.

"Fine," Amado said simply.

"Has he gotten over that dressing down he got in the street?"

Amado winced. "I guess so. He hasn't said anything about it." His face became apprehensive. It was plain that he was afraid the priest was listening from the concealment of the garden. "I guess you've got to go," said Tony, relenting.

"Yes," said Amado quickly. He said good-bye and made a short wave, still managing not to look directly at Tosca.

Tosca's head was bent pensively as they walked along. "You were mean to Amado. Don't you like him?"

Tony's brows knitted. "I used to like him. But I don't very much any more. I used to feel sorry for him because he was afraid of everything. Now he's almost a man and he still acts like a kid."

It was Tosca's turn to be quiet.

Tony glanced at her. "You better leave him alone," he said, divining her thoughts. "He's going to be a priest."

"He hasn't made up his mind. Maybe he doesn't want to be a priest. Maybe he wants to be a singer, and get rich and have a beautiful wife."

"If he wants to be a singer, he's got to leave his mother and the priest and this town. He hasn't got enough guts to do that."

"If you're so brave, why did you come back?"

Tony flushed. "That's my business."

"Well, don't get mad, I was just teasing. I know you came back because of me."

What he almost said would not have been pretty. Reminding himself of Smale Calder's detachment, he decided to keep his mouth shut. There were times when ignoring a situation was the best answer after all.

As though reading his silence, she said, "Do you like Smale Calder?"

Tony was startled. "I don't know him that well."

"You like him because nobody else likes him. I can understand that."

She was getting too close to his thinking and Tony resented it. "But he doesn't ask anybody to like him," he said evasively. "All he wants is to be left alone. He goes right on doing what he wants to, and he doesn't give a damn what they think. He's just not afraid of them."

"Who do you mean by 'them'?"

"I mean everybody. I mean the whole world."

"Is that why you came back, Tony? Because you were afraid?" Instantly, she knew she had gone too far. She caught his arm. "I'm sorry," she pleaded. "I didn't mean that."

But Tony was too stunned by the confrontation to be angry. He had told himself all sorts of things, that he had come back because his brothers had gone, that he should stay at home for at least a while, and even that he did not want to go away from the town. He knew now that none of it was the truth, and that he was afraid to go back into the world. And this was the reason he did not like Amado any more, because he saw in him the same kind of fear.

He looked about him, seeing for the first time in as long as he could remember the familiar scenes with which he had grown up. They were coming to a farm, and even before he saw the oven, the smell of burning wood and the fragrance of new bread came to him. A farm woman, her broad face flushed with the heat that poured out of the stone oval, paused only long enough to wave and call to them in her strong man's voice and then went back to her task of shoveling the bread tins out of the oven with a long-handled platter.

They made their way through the chickens that were pecking aimlessly about the yard, past the stone farmhouse, where the children peeped out from behind the big, open windows. One boy, older than the rest, stood in the doorway and smirked knowingly at them, and they looked away in a common guilt.

When they had passed the pigpen with its snuffling chorus of sounds, and the old skeletons of horse wagons and hand plows that stood behind the house, they were in the open fields again and coming to the river. Because all of this was familiar, it was not fearful. At last, Tony knew that the reason did not lie here either. It was hidden within himself.

They lay side by side on a patch of grass that sloped gently to the river, in an enclosure of willows that shut them off from the world. From the bottom land across the river the scent of dead leaves carried to them with the beginning breeze.

"No, I'll go away, all right," he said aloud. "But only when I'm ready to go, and not before."

Tosca had long since forgotten what it was that they had been talking about. She was nearly asleep in the warmth of the last sun that filtered through the cottonwoods. There was one thing she had not forgotten, though, and the pleasure of her knowledge reflected in her sleeping face.

Tony lay on his side and watched her, until his own anticipation made its drugged way through his limbs and made his breathing difficult. She had unbuttoned her blouse, and from where he lay he could see the whiteness of a nippled breast in its uncertain hiding place. Stretching out his hand, he slipped it under her blouse and cupped it over her breast. Her eyelids fluttered, but she did not move. He began to stroke her gently, and her breathing grew faster. But she did not turn to him until her breast had grown warm with inner heat and she was trembling.

# 6

THE ECHOES OF HIS OWN SCREAM lingered in the room. Father Savio Lazzaroni lay stiff with dread in the utter darkness. In the void above his staring eyes, the brilliant vision of the wheatfield faded and grew and faded and grew with each loud pulsing of his heart, becoming less brilliant and less clear with each beat. He lay without daring to think or even to move, letting the dream die of its own accord, terrified that the least exertion of thought might make it a reality.

When at last the dream had faded to nothing and there was only blackness, he raised a trembling hand to his face. His flesh was cold to his own touch, but he had made the connection and he felt that he would be safe. After a while he forced his stunned sensibilities to propel his legs out of the bed and stand him on his feet and carry him across the stone floor to the light switch. In an instant, the room was transformed from blackness to glaring light.

Moving out of memory, because it was not the first time that it had happened this way, he shambled weakly across the room and lighted the holy candles beside his bed. Their warm glow was reassuring to him, and he turned off the electric light and came back to kneel before them in the prayer chair that had been his mother's. His first prayers were only mumbled repeatings of words that had lost their meaning. As he uttered them, he imagined he felt a palpable presence forming in the shadows of the room behind him, and he covered his face with his hands and began to moan, "Oh my God please protect me from him in my weakness, Oh my God please protect me from him, Oh my God please protect me from him."

Because it would be forever frozen out of all remembering, he did not know how long he prayed and how he had prayed. But in the end he realized dimly that the shivered coursing of his back had stopped, and he saw through his tear-wet fingers that there was a gray light in the room. Still he did not move until in the beginning light a cock crew and he knew the day had come and night had passed.

There was a bench outside the house that faced the morning sun, and Father Savio sat on the cold stone and watched the breaking of the day. The lights in the distant farmhouses winked off one by one, and in the town there was smoke rising from the chimneys of early-wakening families. The sun cleared the rim of the mountains and finally came to bathe the front of the house with light and warmth.

That he had dreamed the dream was no surprise to him now. All the evening before he had known that it would return that night. He had heard the distant bell note of warning at the moment that Amado told him the story of what had happened in the desert between the man and the serpent.

## 61 §

When Amado had gone and the warning grew stronger within him, he had in his fright clung even to the presence of Mrs. Ricco. Long after the dinner was done and her duties taken care of, he had struggled to keep her talking, until finally she was asleep in her chair and he had had to surrender and wake her up and tell her to go home.

He knew now that he had been doubly deceived. It was not in him to fear a man, and yet, unexplainably, he feared Smale Calder. It was not in him to hate a man, and yet after the humiliation of the quarrel in the public street he had been consumed by hatred. Then the dream had come. That it was ordained he was certain. And it must have come to show him the truth. But of this he was for an instant less certain.

He remembered that in the dream he had peered more closely to see the face of the man in the wheatfield. It had seemed very important that he should see the face of the man. And though the shape of the man had become clearer than before, he had seen nothing of the face before the moment of screaming, that moment when the realization of the dream itself struck his senses with a horror as fresh as when he had dreamed it the first time.

That the face had not finally come clear to him was perplexing, because he knew in the depths of his being that it was also ordained he should one day see the face of the man in the wheatfield. When he considered this, he could come to no answer, because it seemed so very obvious that the face should now have come clear. And yet, it had not.

He struggled vainly with the problem, and then in his weariness satisfied himself that the mystery was of God's design, and that it would be revealed to him in its proper time.

So, in this little town of no importance, he and the man and the dream had become linked, as they must have been destined to do from the beginning. And here, too, the thing would at last be resolved.

They were coming as a delegation, and Manuel Cafferata was not surprised. From the window of his office he saw them standing together in front of Della Santa's bank, shoring up their purpose before stepping into the street.

As delegations went, it was a good one, the schemer flanked on one side by holiness and on the other by strength. There was Della Santa, dapper and sure of himself, tapping his cane on the sidewalk to emphasize what he was saying to the other two. There was Father Savio, paler than usual and looking like a gaunt scarecrow in his black priest's suit. And there was Giometti, listening in rapt attention with his powerful butcher's hands on his hips and his bull neck bowed.

"I told you it was going to happen," Joe Morelli said.

"You didn't have to tell me," said Manuel Cafferata. "I been around long enough to know when to expect a delegation."

"I knew it was going to happen when I heard the sermon in church last Sunday. Like everything else he says, it didn't make sense. But I could tell it meant trouble."

"You never did explain what you were doing in church, Morelli."

Morelli shrugged. "It was Tosca's saint day. So the wife cried until I said I would go."

## 63 §

Manuel Cafferata was in a sense relieved. He had believed for a moment that Della Santa had conceived the plan, and it worried him that the banker was getting smarter in his ways to embarrass Cafferata. But it had not been Della Santa's idea after all. The priest had planted the germ in his mind.

When the delegation came in the door, Cafferata turned his back on them and purposely sat down at his desk before saying hello. It was not much of an insult to Della Santa, who weighed Cafferata with a sardonic smile, but at least it was an insult.

"Don't you stand up when a priest comes in the room?" said Della Santa, trying to turn it back.

Cafferata waved his hand. "Father Savio and I know each other well enough not to worry about things like that. Isn't that so, Father?"

"Of course," the priest said, with a quick, nervous smile that showed he was thinking of something else.

Joe Morelli moved to the door. "This looks like private business, Manuel. I think I will take a walk."

"Stay around," said Cafferata, knowing that Joe Morelli's presence was disturbing to Della Santa. "We got no secrets here."

Giometti saw the joke and made the mistake of laughing. Della Santa glanced at him savagely, and Giometti hunched his shoulders and hung his head like a child. Motioning them to the visitors' chairs against the wall, Cafferata said elaborately, "What can I do for you?"

Della Santa neither sat down nor acknowledged Cafferata's question. He could not bear to sit when he had something important to say. Waving his thin cane slightly in front of him, he began to pace back and forth as if in deep thought. For several minutes, the only sound in the office was the occasional tap of his cane and the ticking of the clock on the wall.

Joe Morelli could not support it any longer. "Sit down, Della Santa. You're making me nervous."

It was an unexpected attack, and Della Santa whirled on him. "You can't talk to me like that."

"The hell I can't. I don't owe you no money. I would rather steal it than borrow it from you."

"What I hear from the farmers, I could say something about stealing," said Della Santa.

"Well, don't do it," said Manuel Cafferata. "If you got something on your mind, tell it to me."

Della Santa leaned across Cafferata's desk. "I'll tell you something, all right. You're in bad trouble this time."

When Manuel Cafferata spoke, it was in a voice that was quiet with warning. "You talk to me in anger, you keep your hands off my desk."

Della Santa straightened, regarding Cafferata with a little returning of the old respect. It was enough to allow him to regain control of himself. He began without emotion, as if he were telling a story. "When my working day is over, my wife and I like to go out and sit in our garden. Now we can't do that. Whenever we walk around or sit down, we are afraid one of those rattlesnakes that the American has in his pen has gotten loose and is hiding where we can't see him. It's the same way with everybody in this town, and you are doing nothing about it. Do you even know how many he has got in there now?"

"Sure, I know," said Cafferata.

"He has got five rattlesnakes in that pen. And he is going to have more. He has even got the farmers helping him out. Instead of killing the snakes in their fields, they are sending for this man Calder to come and get them, just so they can see him pick them up in his bare hands."

"What can I do? There's no law against it in this town."

Della Santa looked pained. "There's no law for or against anything in this town, except what you decide. In fact, we are not even a town. If we were a town like it should be, we would have elections and we would have a government, and we wouldn't have toilets in outside houses. We could keep some of the taxes we give as a present now to the people in the county seat so that they can have inside toilets and streets that are paved."

Father Savio, who had been leaning forward in his chair, stirred restlessly. "This isn't what we came to talk about," he said in a strained voice.

Manuel Cafferata had stood up and was puffing in his anger. "You don't fool me, Della Santa," he said, ignoring the priest. "You are just trying to make trouble for me, and you are using these men to help you get what you want. You want this chair. But I tell you, Della Santa. You're not big enough of a man to sit in it."

The priest's mouth trembled as he spoke. "I am not being used in this matter. I am here of my own free will. I would be here if Della Santa did not exist, because I know that something must be done about this evil man and his serpents."

Joe Morelli had been watching Father Savio intently. He

had never considered him seriously before, but ever since the priest had come into the room his manner had given Morelli pause. Now, in the unbelieving silence that followed the priest's words, a piece of the puzzle fell into place. Joe Morelli felt an unaccustomed chill at the base of his spine.

Della Santa cleared his throat noisily. "I understand what you are trying to say, Father," he said, without conviction. "But things such as that are Church matters. What we want to talk about today is the fact that this man Calder is keeping a den of rattlesnakes in this town, and Cafferata is doing nothing about it."

Father Savio was not to be put aside. "I don't expect you to understand until you see the proof of it with your own eyes. It is given for only some of us to see. I am warning you that this man must be destroyed, or else it will be too late for all of us."

Even then Della Santa would have tried again to salvage the purpose for which they had come. Before he could speak, Giometti cried emphatically, "That's the same way I feel, Father. There's got to be something wrong with a man who likes rattlesnakes." After that, Della Santa did not even bother to say good-bye.

# 7

SYMPATHY WAS AN EMOTION THAT had never troubled Joe Morelli much. It was a luxury that one could not afford in the business of living, at least until the time had come when a man was either so rich or so old that he could indulge a weakness. As things stood, Joe Morelli was neither too old nor nearly rich enough for his own liking. Yet, when Manuel Cafferata had gone out the door and Joe Morelli had watched his squat figure trudging off down the street, he had felt a sympathy for him.

It was an emotion that disturbed Joe Morelli as much by the fact that it was alien to him as that he could waste it on another man. If Cafferata should get in trouble, Joe Morelli had always thought he would be the first to make sure that the trouble was serious. He had never deceived himself that it would be otherwise, or for that matter, should be otherwise.

Now the time had finally come when Cafferata was in trouble, and Joe Morelli felt a sympathy for him. It must be, he told himself, that there are not many men in the world who are big enough to deserve sympathy, but Manuel Cafferata is big enough.

The tragic thing about it all was that Cafferata did not know he was in that much trouble. Either he was too old to see it as clearly as he should, or he had a blind spot in him that Joe Morelli had not detected before. Perhaps the whole affair about the snakes was foolish, and didn't make any sense when one thought about it, but foolish affairs that didn't make any sense were usually the ones that caused the most trouble.

The proof was in the delegation. When religion took sides, it was time to watch out. And even though the delegation's intent had fallen apart because of the things the priest had said, Joe Morelli did not deceive himself that it had ended there. The priest was Manuel Cafferata's real enemy.

If the affair of the snakes did lead to trouble, Della Santa was the one who would profit from it. Although his ambition to be the boss of a town was behind it all, what he had said about Cafferata's failures was also the truth. When Cafferata had built the town, he had had exactly his own idea of what it should be like. Because he had been beaten by the unfamiliar world outside, he had tried to make the town as much as possible like the old country that was familiar to him. And he had had exactly his own idea of what a mayor should be, too, and it did not call for such things as elections and town governments and all the complications that went with them. It had worked for a long time, at that. But now it was not working any more, and the town was dying, and all of them knew in their hearts that the new time was coming.

As Joe Morelli had anticipated, Manuel Cafferata was not

long in returning. He came back up the street and into the office looking more weary than when he had left. He did not speak to Joe Morelli or even bother to take off his black hat, but closed the door and went slowly around the desk and sat down with it still on his head.

After a while he sighed deeply. "I'm tired, Joe Morelli."

Joe Morelli did not turn in his chair to look at him. "What did Calder say?"

Cafferata shrugged. "I can't understand the man. He acted like he didn't know what I was talking about. And he meant it, by God. He made me feel like I was asking about what was none of my business. What do you do with a man like that?"

"You could tell the people not to go there any more." Joe Morelli knew as he said it that this was no longer possible.

Manuel Cafferata also knew this was no longer possible. But he said, anyway, "If it comes to that, I will do it. But I'm not sure it would be right. The man has done no wrong." He spread his palms apart. "All right, so it does make you feel funny to see those snakes. But no matter what Della Santa says, they couldn't get out of that pen if they wanted to, and the crazy thing is, it doesn't look to me like they want to."

Joe Morelli did not answer. He sat looking out the window in silence. The day was ending, and the street was darkening with the first dusk. He watched the lights go out in the bank across the square. Della Santa came out and locked the door. He glanced once at the mayor's office, then went up the street toward his house.

"The priest is your enemy, Manuel."

Manuel Cafferata looked up, startled. "What are you talking about, Joe Morelli?"

It was costing Joe Morelli to say it. "What I am telling you, I am telling you from my heart."

Cafferata had never heard Joe Morelli speak in such a manner, and he was touched. "You shouldn't talk like that about a priest," he said, with an embarrassed laugh.

Joe Morelli had said as much as he was going to say. In the gloom of the office, the massive profile of his face was etched like stone against the lighter gloom outside the window.

Manuel Cafferata chuckled again in a prolonging of his gentle rebuke. It was an empty sound, because there was with it a return of the helplessness that was no stranger to him, as if a baffling something had come into the room and lay in the darkness just outside his comprehension.

"From the beginning, the devil has walked among men. The history of the Church is filled with the stories of his black visitations upon earth. He has not come among us with a forked tail and a cloven hoof, by which signs man has come to think of him. Instead, he has taken strange shapes and forms to hide himself and work his evil on our souls so that we could not suspect him until it was too late. To the Garden of Eden he came disguised as a serpent. He has also come among us in the shape of a man, so that it has not always been easy to recognize him. But though he may hide himself from us in the shape of a man, he cannot hide the evil in his soul. He cannot hide the signs by which the righteous can recognize him."

## 71 §

From his vantage point on the side of the altar, Amado glanced from time to time at the people and wondered how much of the sermon was getting through to them. By their faces, it was impossible to tell. To Della Santa perhaps, because the priest had said it openly in Cafferata's office. But even Della Santa's expression was one of veiled disapproval, because he had already chastised the priest for having gone too far.

There was an impassiveness in the sun-blackened faces of the farmers who had come to Mass, looking as always a little strangled in their Sunday suits, and a simple pleasure in the coarse faces of the farm women in their delicate black head scarves. For them, this was their hour of peace after the hard work of a week, and they were conscious only of being dressed up and being in the company of other people who were dressed up, and of having the chance to sit in silence and let the play of rich vestments and golden chalices and droning Latin soothe them with a sense of luxury.

"One of these signs by which his presence can be known is the change that the devil works among men." Amado turned his attention to the gaunt figure of the priest. "Without their being aware of it, he arouses in them a lust for the unclean and the unnatural, and so lures them to evil thoughts and deeds. He places temptation in their path. He sets men against each other so that they cannot see what is happening to them, until it is too late."

Amado felt a return of his own inadequacy. How could he hope to be a priest if he could not recognize and know evil when he saw it? Father Savio had said the man Smale Calder was evil, but Amado was helpless to recognize it. On the occasions when Calder had come into the store, Amado had watched him closely to see the workings of evil. Calder acted as if he were unaware of anybody else's presence. Amado had even tried to talk to him, but each time there had been in Calder's face a surprise, because his privacy had been interrupted. He had answered only what needed to be answered, and then he had retreated again into his aloneness.

Yet, Amado could see that Calder had worked changes in men and set them against each other, as the priest had said. Manuel Cafferata had changed. He had suddenly seemed to become an old man who was confused about things, and kept to his office so as not to show it. His enemies had sensed this, and now they were speaking openly against him, and Della Santa had thrown away his caution like a hungry bird. The butcher, Giometti, was sullen and brooding, and even Tony had set aside his flamboyance and was hostile and quiet, as if he were watching everyone with judging eyes.

Thinking of Tony, Amado thought about himself, and looked covertly at where Tosca Morelli was sitting. She must have been anticipating what he was going to do. Her gaze was full upon him, and her mouth was parted expectantly. The blood rushed into Amado's face, and he fixed his attention quickly on the floor in front of him.

With a stab of guilt, he wondered if Father Savio had divined the change that was happening in him, too. In the priest's obsession with Smale Calder and the snake pen, it did not seem possible that he was concerned with anything else. But how could Amado know that for certain?

It had begun unexpectedly, and for no reason that he could think of. For weeks now, and it had been growing worse each day, his nights were filled with thoughts of Tosca Morelli. It had become so that he could not bear to look at her, and yet he could not keep his eyes away from her, either. When it started, he had tried desperately to wash the impurity of his desires away with prayer. But the fact that prayer had failed did not terrify him as much as the knowledge that he had wanted it to fail.

"From the first dawn of man's creation, the serpent has been the symbol of evil," said Father Savio. "From that day of downfall, the serpent has been hated and feared by all. It is not only that he is a cold-blooded creature in a world of warm-blooded animals. It is not only that he lies silently and in waiting, and that his sting is death. He is the creation of the devil, and his sting is the death of the soul. He is the devil's instrument. He is the unnatural thing that is alien to mankind. Know him by his presence. If there is a man among you for whom the serpent is not alien, then know him, too, by his presence."

## 8

THEY WENT OUT INTO THE DESERT when the dawn was only a pale wash of light against the purple of the night sky. Their destination was the base of a distant rimrock, where Smale Calder said a man could sometimes find a whole den, if he were lucky.

When they had driven as far as they could with the truck, they left it at the road's end and continued on foot. For a long time the only sound in the great silence was the crunch of sand beneath their feet and the dry swishing of sagebrush against their ankles. The sun came up as they were walking, and soon the chill was gone out of the air. The desert was bathed with the first gentle warmth of the day.

They had climbed to the crest of a little knoll when Smale Calder's hand suddenly stretched out in a signal. Tony stopped short in his tracks, tinglings of uncertainty playing up and down his legs. But whatever had attracted Calder was at a distance. "Unless I'm dead wrong," he said quietly, "you're going to see a sight that not many men get a chance to see." He gestured with his hand. "Get down on the ground and don't move."

Tony flattened down beside Smale Calder on the crest of the knoll. They lay on the sand, so that even their heads were concealed by the sagebrush and they were peering through the gaps in the branches. Below them, stretching out from the knoll, was a broad open space of white sand that caught the first sunlight as in a pocket. Rimmed about by sagebrush, it was like a tiny amphitheater.

Tony searched the open sand with his eyes and, when he saw nothing, glanced questioningly at Calder. The man lay propped on his elbows, so that his big head and its cap of brown lank hair jutted out grotesquely. He pursed his lips in a warning. Tony turned back to the sand pit, resting his chin on his crossed wrists, and waited.

When the first rattlesnake, and then the second, coming from another direction an instant later, glided soundlessly out of the sagebrush and into the open space of sand, an involuntary gasp escaped from Tony. But if Smale Calder heard, he did not show it. He was frozen in immobility.

As methodically as they had come into the amphitheater, the snakes paused and their heads raised up. They regarded each other across the intervening space of sand, and then one of them rattled faintly, and the other followed suit. The sound was different, not like any rattling Tony had ever heard. It was not angry, but like a greeting. As soon as it was accomplished, they lowered their heads and glided toward each other.

When they met in the center of the amphitheater, they

lay with their heads so close together that they seemed to be touching with their flickering tongues. Then slowly they placed their heads side by side and, in unison, began to rise from the ground in a movement so fluid that it did not have a beginning.

Their heads still touching, and their bodies leaning against each other, they rose slowly into the air until they were supported only by their tails. When they had reached as high as they could, the upward movement stopped and their necks slipped around each other, locked in an embrace. Then, with a suddenness that struck Tony's forehead in a wave of shock, the fluid motion erupted into lashing fury. In an instant, one of the snakes had been hurled to the ground so violently that the thump came audibly to their ears. He lay stunned, the white of his underbelly showing, and then he righted himself. The other snake, coiled loosely on the ground, watched him with slightly raised head but did not pursue his advantage.

Five more times, in which Tony lost all awareness of where he was and what he was doing, the snakes went through the ritual of coming together, rearing slowly into the air, and locking necks in embrace, only to burst apart with blinding swiftness.

When it was all over, they separated as if in mutual accord and quit the amphitheater, each going away in the direction from which he had come. Smale Calder rose and brushed the sand from his shirtfront.

Tony got up as far as his knees and sat back weakly on his haunches. "God almighty."

"You can say that again," Calder muttered. "It was a real

scrap. The gray one had too much strength for him, though."

"For a while I didn't know it was a fight. I thought they were screwing."

Calder glanced down at him with amusement. "Yeah, I guess that's right. It's been a while, but I remember thinking that, too, when I was a kid."

"It's a wonder they didn't kill each other."

Calder shook his head. "Naw, they never do. Rattlers are funny that way. They get something going between them and they wrestle it out. But I've never seen one get killed, or even hurt bad, for that matter. Fact is, they'll quit if there's a sign of hurt. Most times, they're just plain satisfied with a draw."

Without knowing why it came to mind, Tony said, "I saw Giometti fight a man once in the saloon. When he got him down was when he really tried to hurt him. He would have killed him if the others hadn't stepped in then."

"A lot of men don't seem satisfied with just having it out," Calder said. "If there was nothing to stop them, I guess they'd kill every time." He began to move off the knoll. "Let's get that gray before he's gone for good."

As he followed Smale Calder's rough advance through the sagebrush, it occurred to Tony that he was beginning to take many things for granted that would have made him doubt his senses before. Now the fact that they were going after a rattlesnake and that he was going to stand by placidly while Calder captured him with his bare hands seemed perfectly normal to him. And yet, when he had been a boy and the others had made pets of watersnakes and blue racers, he had never wanted to, because he was afraid of them. In the time he had been with Smale Calder, it had gotten to the point where he could pass the snake pen in the yard without even noticing that it was there. It was curious how living with snakes in plain sight, and beginning to know a little about them, could change one's ideas. What it amounted to was seeing an old fear in a new light, or putting it in its proper place. *I wonder if because of this strange man and his snakes,* thought Tony, *I am finally beginning to understand myself.*

The gray rattlesnake was aware of their approach. Instead of recoiling, however, he was bent on escape. When he knew that he could not escape, he found refuge under a thick clump of sagebrush. Calder made his way to the bush and stood over it. Tony lingered back when he heard the warning rattle.

"He's sure tuckered out," said Calder. "He can barely get enough strength to rattle." Pausing with a thought, Calder turned to Tony. "You want to try taking him?" he said. "With all the fight gone out of him, you couldn't have a better chance to try it out."

Tony backed away. "No, sir," he said firmly. "That's not for me. Maybe I'm not so afraid of them any more. As long as they keep their distance, I'll live with them and I won't bother them. They can go their way, and I'll go mine. I'm not reaching into a bush for any rattlesnake that's hiding there, I don't care how tired he is."

"Yeah, you're right. There's no sense in hunting for trouble. If you don't understand a snake, the best thing to do is leave him lie." Calder turned his back on Tony. "It was just a thought."

Tony remained perfectly quiet while Smale Calder got down on his knees and began his singsong talking to the rattlesnake in the bush. As always, he was entranced by the ritual. But he had also come to realize that it was not a trick of singsong that made Calder able to handle rattlesnakes. That was part of it, of course, but there was something else that was the real reason, and it had to do with fear, or the lack of it, and an understanding between the man and the snake.

Because Smale Calder said there would be no trouble, Tony walked beside him as they made their way back to the truck. The gray snake was cradled on Calder's broad forearms. Still, Calder kept one hand resting behind the snake's head.

"Why do you do that?" Tony asked. "You know he's not going to bite you."

"I don't know that. He's a new snake, and he's still afraid of me. So there's no sense in taking a chance. There's death in that head, and it takes a fool not to know it."

"Are you afraid of him, too?"

"No. If he thought I was afraid of him, he wouldn't be where he is now. When a snake knows you're afraid, then he gets afraid, too. And that's when he'll strike you."

In the distance, over the gray tops of the sagebrush, the truck came into view. The sun was well up over the rim of the mountains now and the desert was bright and clean with the new day. "Is that why the brute snake is so mean," Tony asked, "because he's afraid?"

"The brute snake isn't mean," Calder said. "He's just about the cruelest thing that ever lived. But he's not mean like a rat, if you know what I mean."

"Isn't he afraid at all?"

"So far as I can see, that snake's not afraid of anything.

But at the same time, he knows more about fear than any snake I ever had. He's just waiting to see it in me."

Tony felt a shiver. "Then why do you keep him?"

Smale Calder laughed. "I'll be damned if I know. Maybe it's just because of that." Then, more seriously, he said, "But I think it's because he's such a beautiful thing. You've seen it when the sun hits him. He turns to gold. If there's beauty in this world, that snake is it."

Angelo Ricami, the barber, was not the first to see it, but he was the first to tell about it. Tony had known what was going on, but ever since he heard about the delegation going to see Manuel Cafferata, he said nothing, because the people would not understand. Pasquale had known of it, too, and once or twice in the saloon he started to tell about it. Nobody paid any attention to him, so he gave up trying to explain.

It was a Sunday afternoon when Angelo Ricami, quite by accident, saw that which made his hair stand on end, as he later recounted to everyone who came into his barbershop. He had been to Mass in the morning, and afterward went to Piumbo's saloon for an *aperitivo*. Because he was a widower and could not expect his dinner to be waiting for him at home, he ate expansively at Garzoni's restaurant. Pleasantly stuffed and smoking a good cigar, he was strolling home to take a nap before his drowsiness wore off.

He had passed Smale Calder's garage, which was closed, and was turning the corner, when he saw a movement in the bushes beside the street. There was a high wooden fence connecting the garage to the house, and it shielded the yard. As he looked closer, Angelo Ricami saw that it was the boy,

## 81 §

Luigi. He was crouched against the fence, peering through a crack between the old boards. Ricami would have gone on except that he saw the boy was trembling with excitement. His curiosity aroused, he walked over to the fence and stood over the boy. "What you doing, Luigi?"

Luigi started at the sound of Ricami's voice. He looked up balefully and hissed, "Shut up!"

If it had been anybody else, Ricami would have taken offense. But because it was Luigi, and everyone knew he was not quite there, Ricami ignored what he said. "What you looking at, boy?" he whispered, and then stooped over to peer through the fence, too.

It was a moment before his mind told him what his eyes were seeing. When it did, his breath left him in a rush. He backed away from the fence so quickly that he almost fell into the weeds. Luigi, still glued to the crack, made a furious motion for silence. Ricami's first impulse was to shout, until he realized there was no one to shout for. He stood breathing heavily for a while, and then went back to the fence and stooped over the boy to look again.

The scene in the yard was being enacted in utter silence. The stranger, Smale Calder, was down on his knees in the snake pen, and his legs and arms and chest were alive with rattlesnakes. There were so many that their coils were interwound with each other. At first Ricami thought they were twisting to be free from Smale Calder's grasp, and then he saw that they were writhing over each other to climb higher in his arms. One had reached upward so high that his head was on a level with Calder's, and his darting black tongue was almost touching the man's lips. It occurred to Ricami that the man and the snake were kissing, and the thought made him sick.

But as he watched, he saw that Calder seemed to be blowing at the snake's head. Each time that he did, the snake would jerk away, and then return. Finally, Calder reached one hand up gently and took the snake by the neck and, extricating him from the rest, set him down on the ground. He lay there for an instant, rattled once as if in mild irritation, and then turned and glided peacefully away to his den in the rocks.

There was one snake, however, that had not joined the others. It was the brute snake that Ricami had seen once before, when he had come with Piumbo to have a look at the pen. That time, Ricami had caught only a glimpse of him inside his rock cave. This time he was fully revealed, coiled halfway between his den and Smale Calder, so that the sun glinted off his golden scales. He was not participating in what was going on, but seemed to be a spectator, instead. Ricami noticed that every once in a while Calder would turn away from the others to gaze at the brute snake, and that in those moments the bemused child's expression on the man's face would fade away, and he would become sober.

Ricami stayed at the crack in the fence until he realized that his dinner was not resting easily. He straightened with a grunt that made the boy at his feet glance up quickly. This time, however, Luigi was not angry. His face was alight, and he was smiling radiantly. Ricami did not pay attention to it at the time because he was filled with an excitement of his own. He made his way back to Piumbo's saloon for a drink to settle his stomach. Already, he was framing in his mind how best to enlarge upon what he had seen.

## 83 §

The curious thing about it all was that no one thought to ask Smale Calder himself if the story were true. While the news licked through the town and the farms, he was perfectly oblivious of what was happening. He went on about his business in the garage, ignoring the appraisals of those who came in for gasoline and repairs, and even the open-mouthed regard of the children who peeked in the doorway to catch a glimpse of him.

The news made the turn of the town and the farms three times. Angelo Ricami's was the first version, and since he was a good storyteller, it was the best. He held court in his barbershop, and he exacted a profit from it.

"Already I have wasted enough time telling this for nothing," he said to the men who were crowded inside. "Why should I take my working day to tell you? Even if it's a fine story that should be told, I got to make a living, too."

Choosing his field, Ricami settled upon a farmer named Longo, who had notoriously fast-growing whiskers. "But it's not the end of the week," Longo argued. "I promise you, though, that I will come in Saturday."

"So why don't you surprise your wife on Tuesday by looking like a man instead of a bear," said Ricami.

When Longo finally gave in and Ricami had him safely in the barber chair, he went on. "There he was with his whole body covered with snakes, and the big brute one on top of all of them."

"That's not what you said yesterday," a farmer named Del Curto interrupted. "Luchetti told me you said the brute snake was watching."

Deciding that Del Curto would be the next man who would have a shave before his time, Ricami said, "Who should know best, Luchetti or me? Was Luchetti there to see it?"

Del Curto would have liked to argue the point but, sensing what was in Ricami's mind, fell silent with the hope that the story would be done before it became his turn for a shave.

"Of all the strange sights I have seen in my wide experience," Ricami said, "this was the most unbelievable. There, before my eyes, I saw the brute snake raise himself up until his head was even with Calder's. And then the snake kissed the man right on the lips!"

There was a commotion near the door. Ricami stopped in surprise. It was Giometti, and he was trying to force his way out of the barbershop. "What's the matter, Giometti?" the barber called out to him. "Don't you like my story?"

Giometti did not look well. "I don't believe it!" he shouted.

"But it's true. I swear on my mother," said Ricami. "That brute snake put his tongue right on Calder's mouth."

At this, Giometti's eyes rolled upward and he turned a sickly hue. The men in the barbershop roared with enjoyment, and Giometti groped his way blindly through the door into the street.

Still, because Ricami was a gossip and given to bending the truth, not everybody believed him. And when the story took more elaborate turns with each telling, there were many who began to think he had made up the whole incident. It would not have been the first time he had preyed on their imaginations as a practical joke.

Then Pasquale confirmed the story, and added a few facts of his own, and for a while was the center of attention in Piumbo's saloon.

"This is nothing new to me. I have seen it many times,"

he said patronizingly, although the truth of the matter was that he had witnessed it only once, and then accidentally, when he went back to the garage on a Sunday to find a plug of chewing tobacco he had forgotten there.

"Then Tony must have watched him, too," said Piumbo. "And if he has, why won't he say so?"

"Maybe he hasn't," said Pasquale. "He has not watched it when I have been there, at least. But then, Calder has made it clear that he has favored me to watch because he knows I'm not a big mouth, like some barbers I know."

"When does he do this thing?" asked Garzoni, who had come over from his restaurant with his apron on.

Pasquale was taken aback for only a moment. "On Sunday afternoons, when everything is quiet," he said, feeling on fairly sure ground since both he and the barber had seen it on separate Sundays. "And holidays, too."

After this, there was doubt again, because nobody had ever taken Pasquale seriously before, and now was no time to start. Also, his story differed from Ricami's in important ways, and no one could be quite sure whether it was because of the barber's habit of exaggerating.

Della Santa finally got to the truth when he went to Tony's house one night and accosted him in front of his mother and father. "You have a duty to the town to tell me," he said, ignoring the young man's hostility.

"Why?" Tony asked. "It's nobody else's business what he does in his own yard."

"Then what you are telling me is that he does do this thing."

"I didn't say that."

"I believe you did, if you think about it," said Della Santa impatiently.

Tony's mother, who was overwhelmed by the fact of the banker's presence in her house, clasped her hands imploringly. "Tony, please. Remember who you are talking to."

Tony looked at her and then at his father, who sat staring at the floor and saying nothing. "All right, so he plays with his own snakes for his own pleasure. I don't expect you can understand that."

Della Santa was suddenly expansive with friendliness. "My boy, how can I understand unless you explain it to me?"

But after he tried to explain, gropingly and with thoughts he had never voiced before, Tony realized that the banker did not understand at all, nor was he interested in understanding.

Della Santa left the house in triumph, though he was not quite sure in his own mind what he was trying to prove. He went to Manuel Cafferata and confronted him with what Tony had said, and was further confused when he saw that Cafferata genuinely did not attach any importance to the whole affair.

"I can't see what you're getting excited about, Della Santa," said Cafferata. "We all knew he could pick up a rattlesnake in his bare hands. What difference does it make if he picks up twenty of them instead of one?"

"But there is a difference," argued Della Santa.

"What difference? Unless you are going to believe that crazy business of Ricami's about the snakes kissing him. You know Ricami better than that."

When Della Santa went to Father Savio's house with the

news, he received still another surprise. The priest heard him with only a grim nodding of his head, as if he had known it had been going on all along.

"Do you think you are telling me anything I haven't already foreseen?" said the priest. "The man is evil, and this is only further proof of it. How clearly does it have to be revealed before the people can understand there is a devil in their midst?"

Della Santa felt himself withdrawing into the incomprehension that the priest's words always seemed to evoke in him. Then, by chance, he looked up to see Mrs. Ricco eavesdropping from the kitchen. The priest's housekeeper crossed herself and covered her eyes, and Della Santa knew that even if he could not divine its meaning, what had happened would somehow work to his advantage.

Because he had once called for Smale Calder to come and capture a rattlesnake that he had flushed out on his farm, it remained for Joe Caneva to do the straightforward thing. He was a simple man, and from that moment he had felt a proprietary right in the snake pen. He could not make it to town for some days after he first heard the story. When he did, he went directly to the garage. Calder was eating his lunch alone in his little house. He came out when Joe Caneva insisted that Pasquale fetch him.

Extending his hand in comradely fashion, Joe Caneva said, "How's our snakes doing? They getting along all right?"

Smale Calder grinned rarely, but he did now. "They're getting along just fine, Joe."

Joe Caneva nodded in satisfaction. "Can I see mine?"

"Sure," said Calder. "This time of day, he's probably asleep. But we can give it a try."

They went out together through the garage. The sun had not yet tipped enough for shade from the cottonwood tree, and the yard was baking hot. As Smale Calder had said, the snakes were hidden away in their rock caves. He circled the pen, arching his neck back and forth, and gestured to Joe Caneva. "There," he said. "You can catch a look at him from here. See him under that brown slab that's got its point up in the air?"

Joe Caneva leaned forward and squinted into the sunlight. "Yeah, that looks like him, all right. But I'll be damned if I'm sure."

"That's him, all right," Calder said with conviction.

Joe Caneva straightened and slowly surveyed the entire pen. "You mean you really get inside there and let those things crawl all over you?"

Smale Calder was startled. "How'd you know that?"

"Oh, everybody is talking about it," Joe Caneva said in a matter-of-fact way. "The barber saw you through the fence. Now everybody is talking about it."

"I don't know why."

"Well, it's not everybody that can do a trick like that." When Smale Calder became thoughtful, Joe Caneva demanded, "You gonna do it again this Sunday?"

"Do what?"

"Why, get in there with them snakes."

Calder shrugged. "I don't know. I guess I will if I get time."

Joe Caneva rubbed his hands in satisfaction. "That's fine. I'll come and watch you, the family and me."

## 89 §

"I don't know about that," Calder said gravely. "I never have done it with people around. I don't know how the snakes will take to something like that." Without being aware of it, his gaze rested for an instant on the huge rock cave where the brute snake was dozing.

"Oh, we'll be quiet," said Joe Caneva. "You won't even know we are here."

"I'm not sure," Calder said doubtfully.

Because he had not said no, Joe Caneva took his answer for yes. With a broad smile that showed his blackened teeth, he shook Calder's hand. "Now, don't you forget to tell me when my snake crawls on you," he said. "I'll probably know him, but I might get mixed up with so many of them."

Before there was a chance for argument, Joe Caneva waved broadly and took his leave. Smale Calder raised his hand to call him back, and then let it drop.

# 9

IT SEEMED TO FATHER SAVIO THAT THE church was more crowded than usual for Sunday Mass. It was an unexpected pleasure that did not fail to give him a lift of heart. For the first time he began to believe that his words were not falling on fallow ground, and even imagined that the faces that looked up at him during the sermon were beginning to show understanding.

He managed to make a quick survey to see who was there that had not been there before. It was the family, or rather, the several families, of Caneva. This puzzled him, and he wondered if it was the death anniversary of someone in the family. But if that were so, he would have been asked to offer up the Mass, and so would have known. Since he had not been asked, the situation made him suddenly ill at ease.

It was not usually Father Savio's custom to mingle with the people as they visited outside the church after Mass. This Sunday, however, he finished his unvesting with a hurry that surprised Amado. In fact, the only word he exchanged with

91 §

Amado was to ask him if he knew why all the Canevas had come to Mass. Amado did not know, and Father Savio promptly ignored him. The priest left the sacristy without even an invitation to Amado for Sunday breakfast.

After Mass was a time of visiting for the townspeople and farmers who had not seen each other for a while. The men gathered in their own little clusters, separated from the talk of the women. Father Savio wandered from one group to another, nodding hello and exchanging a few words, feeling with a familiar rankle the withdrawal that his presence provoked. Though he was their priest, it had always been this way. He knew too much about their secret hearts, and he could not help revealing it in his eyes.

There was an argument going on in a corner of the churchyard. Joe Caneva was the center of it. His hands were waving, and his face was flushed with a color that was not from the sun.

The others did not seem to be angry. Instead, they had grins on their faces, as though they were taking delight in teasing him. The priest moved slowly toward the group. "I am not going to lie to you in front of the church," he heard Joe Caneva say loudly. "Why do you think I have all my family here if I'm not telling you the truth?"

"Now, now, gentlemen," said Father Savio, boldly approaching the men. "We shouldn't argue on Sunday."

The others immediately fell silent, but Joe Caneva was too much in the heat of it to do likewise. "I'm not arguing, Father," he said defensively. "It's them that's making the argument. They're calling me a liar."

"We didn't call you a liar," said one of the men.

"It's the same thing," cried Joe Caneva. "When you don't believe what a man says to you, you're calling him a liar."

Father Savio raised his hands in a gesture of peace. "Now, now, Mr. Caneva. There are times when we misjudge what others think."

"I'm not misjudging them. But they'll be laughing out of the other side of their mouths when they find out I am telling them the truth."

"That may well be true," said Father Savio soothingly. "If it is, then one must be patient and wait for time to prove him right."

"It will, all right," said Joe Caneva. "It damned well will prove it this afternoon. Pardon me, Father."

"If it's any of my business," said Father Savio, with a disguising laugh, "what will prove it this afternoon?"

Glancing wrathfully at the circle of men, Joe Caneva said, "My friend Smale Calder has invited me and my family to let us watch our snakes crawl all over him this afternoon. That's what."

This of all things Father Savio had not been prepared for. He staggered visibly. The men regarded him in astonishment, and even Joe Caneva's anger faded.

The priest's voice was very nearly a scream. "On the Lord's day?"

Joe Caneva's jaw dropped as though it were unhinged. "What's that got to do with it?" he managed to mumble.

"What has that got to do with it?" Father cried. "My God, haven't any of you even understood what I've been trying to tell you?"

## 93 §

They stared at him dumbly. Father Savio looked from one to another of them. Then, abruptly, he wheeled and stumbled through the crowd like a man drunk.

Finally, the noise woke up Smale Calder. He emerged from the house, his lank hair damp from sleeping in the midday heat. He stumbled a little on the wooden stoop, taking in the commotion in the yard with slow-breaking amazement.

Joe Caneva detached himself from the others and came over with hand outstretched, wiping it first on the trousers of his black suit. His mouth was still stuffed with bread and sausage, and he swallowed prodigiously to clear it. "My family," he said simply.

"Your family! Christ, it looks like you got half the town here."

"No. Just my brother, my sisters, and my cousin. Just my family."

"Yeah," said Calder. "And wives and husbands and kids and dogs."

"Well, what you think?" said Joe Caneva, offended.

"I think get those damned dogs away from the snake pen," said Calder, rubbing the top of his head angrily.

Joe Caneva could see reason in this. He bellowed a command at the two mongrel dogs, who, with hackles up, were dancing and yelping in near hysteria around the snake pen. They were in such a state of excitement that they scarcely heard him. Joe Caneva rushed at the closest one and aimed a kick that for the first time in his life struck home. The dog yelped in pain and slunk whimperingly away. His companion joined him, slinking as though he had been kicked, too. There was a shrill burst of laughter from the children, who thought this immensely funny. A word from Joe Caneva silenced them.

"Just like you ordered," he said with broad satisfaction. When Calder did not respond, Joe Caneva's smile faded. He tried another tack. "You look hungry. Why don't you come eat with us?"

Calder shook his head. "I ain't hungry," he said, then added grudgingly when he saw quick insult in Joe Caneva's eyes, "Anyways, I don't eat your kind of food, and the snakes would smell it on me."

Because he had been uncertain that Smale Calder would do as he had promised, Joe Caneva was mollified. "Oh, that's all right, think nothing of it. I understand just what you're saying."

He strode back to the others and announced expansively, "All right, you people, listen to this. My friend Smale Calder is just about ready to get in that pen and let those snakes crawl all over him. So we got to quit eating and talking and be quiet, because it might set them off, and Calder could get bit and maybe even killed."

The men had dragged two long benches from the garage to the shade of the cottonwood tree, seating themselves on one and leaving the other for the women. A tablecloth had been spread on the ground under the tree, and it was stacked with great loaves of bread and open newspapers that held enough garlic sausage and salami and cheese for twice their number. Two gallons of wine, wrapped in wet cloths to keep them cool, still remained untouched, and another, nearly empty, was being passed among the men.

"Christ, Joe," said one who was only a brother-in-law, "all I've had so far is a bite to eat. What's the hurry?"

Joe Caneva threw up his hands. "Because Calder hasn't got all day," he said angrily. "This is something special. If you don't want to see it, you can go somewhere else."

The others, however, did not seem to mind. They finished up their thick sandwiches and washed them down with wine. The gallon was empty, so the brother-in-law brought another one and set it down with a flourish in front of the bench where the men were sitting. Before Joe Caneva could challenge him, he said, "You didn't say anything about drinking. So don't try to say it now."

Joe Caneva shrugged him off in disgust. The women were busy waving away the flies and putting the food back into the carton boxes. The children seated themselves on the ground, whispering and squirming nervously. Joe Caneva raised his hand, and the whispering stopped. The dogs had crept up to a point of safety behind the children, and one of them whimpered.

When the women had gathered themselves in a tight fit on the other bench, Joe Caneva turned to Calder. "Everything is ready." He walked to the men's bench and waited until a place had been made for him in the middle. The new gallon of wine was in front of him. He looked at it longingly for a moment, and then reached down and took a long drink. On the end of the bench his brother-in-law made a sound of contempt.

Smale Calder had been watching the scene in silence. He heaved a great sigh of resignation, but there was still a frown on his brow. He was about to go to the snake pen when a movement in the garage caught his eye. It was the boy, Luigi, hiding in the shadows near the wide door. Calder pointed a finger at him. "You! Get the hell away from here."

Luigi came out of the shadows and began to walk away. To everyone's surprise, because nobody had ever heard of Luigi's crying before, his shoulders were shaking. Smale Calder's anger faded. "You can come back," he called out grudgingly. "But will you for God's sake keep away from the snake pen."

Luigi retraced his steps, staring at Calder with wide eyes that were still bruised with tears. He did not join the others but went to where he had been standing in the shadows near the doorway.

When Calder crossed the yard to the snake pen, one of the women sucked in her breath loudly. Joe Caneva shot her a glance, and then started himself when the dry crackle of an angry rattlesnake came from the snake pen.

It was the brute snake. He had glided out of his rock cave at the same moment Smale Calder began his approach. In the sunlight, he was like a golden sentry, beautiful and deadly.

When Calder's hand hesitated on the gate, the brute snake rattled again, and this time the sound was caught up by the others in the labyrinth of rocks behind him. Then, as suddenly as it had started, the angry hum subsided, and an ominous silence hung over the yard.

Joe Caneva realized that he had been squirming on the bench. He peered sideways at the other men. Their dark faces were drawn as tight as leather, and their eyes were narrowed and watchful. He had seen that expression before, when they had heard the warning of a rattlesnake in their fields.

## 97 §

He looked at the women. Without exception, they had their hands to their mouths, some with knuckles pressed hard against their teeth, others with fingers covering their lips. One of them, his sister, had pinched her nostrils shut. On the ground in front of the bench the children were pale and still, staring ahead with the unblinking, hypnotized eyes of birds.

In the shadows of the garage Luigi was in twitching movement. One hand was raised, and his mouth was working as if he were trying to impart to Smale Calder a knowledge that the others did not possess.

A transformation had come over Calder. The great hulk of his body rose and straightened, and there was a fury in his face like that of a menacing god's. An understanding seemed to pass between him and the brute snake. After a moment the snake slowly uncoiled and retreated into his cave, the sun glinting dully from the golden plates along his back. In the shadows of the garage, the boy's hand dropped. Smale Calder opened the gate and stepped into the snake pen.

For a long time there was no sign of movement in the labyrinth of rocks, even though Calder was calling in low singsong tones. Joe Caneva felt the inquiring eyes of his family upon him, and once, he heard an uncomplimentary sound from his brother-in-law. To his own chagrin, he was beginning to doubt that there was anything to the story after all. Then a rattlesnake pushed its gray length out of the rocks. Smale Calder dropped to his knees in the sand.

There was a certain hesitancy in the movement of the snake. Once he had separated himself from the labyrinth, he stopped and raised his head. His black tongue, with tips spread wide, was flickering in and out of his mouth, as if he were searching for an unseen danger in the air. When he had glided very close, he raised his head again. Calder had not moved, but now he stretched out his hand.

Almost beneath his palm, the snake convulsed into a coil. The whirring of his tail was hysterical in its sound. He jerked his head back, poised in a deadly buttonhook. An agonized cry of warning was torn out of someone in the yard.

Smale Calder remained perfectly still. His outstretched hand hung in the air just above the coiled snake. Time came to a stop in the yard. Then, imperceptibly, the whirring sound subsided into a rustle and finally faded to nothing. The snake raised up slowly, until its darting tongue had touched Calder's open palm. When the man reached out to pick him up, he made no resistance at all.

For a while, he was content to rest in Calder's arms. Then, awakening as from sleep, he pushed himself upward until his head was on a level with the man's. Joe Caneva could see how Ricami, the barber, could have been mistaken. In the beginning, it really did look as though the man and the snake were kissing. But as Joe Caneva watched, he saw that Calder was blowing through his pursed lips at the snake's head, and that the more he did this, the more languid the snake became. By the time Calder set him down to pick up the others who had come out of the rocks and were crawling up his knees and onto his arms and chest, the snake seemed barely to have enough strength to crawl away.

After that, the menace that had hung over the yard disappeared. Even when Calder was covered with moving coils Joe Caneva felt no particular alarm. It all seemed so natural that he found himself wondering which snake was his. He deliberated about approaching the snake pen and asking, and then realized that this would be a foolish thing to do. Although one little corner of Joe Caneva still wished he could have seen the man being bitten by a snake, Smale Calder had come as close to it as anyone could want. And with that, Joe Caneva felt satisfaction enough.

# 10

Manuel Cafferata and Joe Morelli closed the office door behind them and, in common accord, slumped wearily into their chairs. During the time they had been standing in the sun, Joe Morelli had taken off his coat, but Cafferata had refused to, and he could feel the sweat running in streams down his back.

When the coolness had begun to restore him, Manuel Cafferata raised his head to gaze out the window. The street was still thronged with people, but it was not as it had been that morning. The trucks from the farms, their backs loaded with children, were already beginning to go home. The smell of dust churned up by wheels was heavy in the air.

"I never seen anything like it," said Cafferata.

"Well, it's something to see," said Joe Morelli. "But I still think there's a trick to it."

"I'm not talking about that." Cafferata pointed to the street. "I mean that out there. It's like Santa Maria Day every Sunday."

"I wouldn't feel so bad about it. Everybody else is happy.

Piumbo never made so much money in his life. He's even got Pasquale helping him tend bar. Garzoni's restaurant is full every Sunday, and Giometti is making money, too, because Garzoni has got to buy extra meat from him. It's that way all over."

"It must be good for the town at that, I guess," Cafferata said doubtfully.

"If it's good for the town, it's good for you," Joe Morelli said. "It shows you was right in doing nothing about that snake pen. Did you see Della Santa there today?"

"I saw," said Cafferata.

"I wondered how long he was going to stay away. That cost him with the people, his coming today."

"And he was liking it. Did you watch his face?"

Joe Morelli had not watched Della Santa's face, and so he said, "Oh, everybody liked it."

Manuel Cafferata was not quite so sure. He had watched Smale Calder's face, too, and it was plain to him that Calder had not enjoyed himself at all. The calm distance that had marked the man when they met for the first time was not there today. His brow was furrowed, and the eyes that had looked out with detachment before were turned inward today. Cafferata imagined that he saw a slow building anger there. It was as though Calder had been overwhelmed by the demands of the people and that he was showing himself against his will. At one point before he entered the snake pen he had turned and surveyed the yard so packed that nearly everyone was standing in order to see. For an instant it seemed that he would not go in. Manuel Cafferata had thoroughly expected him to tell the people to go home.

"Next, it will be the priest's turn to come," said Joe Morelli. "And then Giometti, and after he has come, you will have the whole town on your side."

"That's not a very good joke. A bad thing is happening to the priest. Did you hear he hasn't given a sermon in three Sundays?"

"No, I didn't hear it," said Joe Morelli, with suddenly veiled eyes. "But then, how could I?"

Manuel Cafferata saw his meaning. "You ought to go to church more often, Joe Morelli," he said seriously. "It don't look good to stay away all the time." He was thoughtful for a moment. "Amado came to see me, you know. He is worried about the priest, because he won't talk to anybody, not even Amado. He has locked himself in that house and he won't come out except for Mass."

Joe Morelli did not share Cafferata's worry. No news that he had heard could have pleased him more. "What did you tell Amado?"

"What could I tell him?" Cafferata threw up his hands. "It's not for me to talk to a priest."

Manuel Cafferata did not choose to tell Joe Morelli about another visit he had had from someone else. But that was because this visit had bothered him more than hearing about the priest's condition. Tony had come to him and, without explanation, begged him to order Smale Calder to stop what he was doing. Cafferata had demanded to know why, but Tony refused to tell him. Cafferata had told him to mind his own business.

Joe Morelli could not leave the subject of the priest alone. "I'll bet you that he will come one of these Sundays. I'll bet that's why Amado was there today. The priest sent him to find out what was going on."

But that was not why Amado was there today, Cafferata reflected. Even if Joe Morelli had been so taken up by the business in the snake pen, Cafferata had kept his eyes open. He knew why Amado had come, and he had not liked knowing it at all.

"Well, when the priest decides to come," Joe Morelli persisted, "then Giometti will come, too. And you will have the whole town on your side."

Manuel Cafferata did not answer him but stared unseeingly out the window. A passing farmer pressed his face against the window pane and waved in greeting. Cafferata raised his hand distractedly. By chance, his gaze had come to rest on Giometti's figure across the street. The butcher was closing up his shop. One would have thought Giometti would be happy with the money he had made this day. But obviously he was not, and it was clearly written in his forbidding manner. The fact that Giometti had made money had nothing at all to do with the awful dread he had for the snake pen, and the realization of this was a confirming of Manuel Cafferata's disquiet.

The only reservation in Amado's mind had been that his going to the snake pen would be the cause of attention. It was the first time that he had gone, and he was practically the only one in town who had not seen Smale Calder's handling of the snakes.

His decision to go had not been difficult. In his rebellion against Father Savio for shutting himself off from the town,

Amado had felt spite against the priest for having included him, too. He had found a certain pleasure in making up his mind to witness what the priest had convinced him was a devil's rite.

When he joined the procession of people who were thronging through the garage, nobody seemed to see anything strange in it. There were no remarks and no glances of curiosity, and Amado saw that their attention was only upon what was going to happen in the snake pen.

When Smale Calder entered the snake pen, Amado forgot his fears. With the others who were standing in the crowded yard, he tensed in anticipation of danger. He was so completely absorbed in Calder's ritual of kneeling and calling to the snakes in the tuneless singsong that he barely felt the touch on his arm. He turned only because the touch was purposeful. With a start he saw that Tosca Morelli was standing beside him.

"Isn't it terrible, Amado?" she whispered. "I'm afraid."

Amado looked about quickly in embarrassment. The faces of the people were oblivious of everything but Smale Calder. As one, they were consumed with the snake pen. When the first of the snakes came out of his rock cave, Tosca clutched at Amado and buried her face against his chest. The touch of her body and the heavy scented fragrance of her hair rose up to smother Amado's senses. From then on, he knew but little of what was happening in the snake pen.

She pushed away from him when the gasps and murmurs of the people told her that the moment had arrived when the snakes were crawling into Calder's arms. If she had been afraid before, Tosca did not reveal it now. Her face was drawn and white with passion. As she watched Calder's fondling of the snakes, she began to breathe quickly, and her breasts pressed out against her blouse so that it seemed it would burst apart.

When Smale Calder was beginning to detach himself from the last of the snakes, Tosca shivered and came awake. She looked up unexpectedly at Amado before he could disguise his want. There was an instant's widening of her eyes. She forced a quick smile. "I'll wait for you outside," she whispered.

Amado waited only a little while after she had gone. Then, with downcast head, he edged his way out of the crowd.

For Amado, it was like being jerked from an unhinged dream into the wakefulness of day. The human smells and lust that had suffocated him began to lift away as soon as he slipped out of the yard. Then the cold knowledge of what he was doing took hold of him.

He faltered and would have gone back to the yard. But he had gone too far. When he looked up, it was to see her waiting for him in the deserted street. If she sensed his hesitation, she did not reveal it. She stood regarding him with an expectancy that was a command.

It was as if the day had been set irrevocably from the beginning, and he was helpless to do anything about it. As he knew she would do, she took him by the hand, and when he felt the contact course like fire through his body, his last resolve crumbled.

"You needn't be so miserable," she said. "I'm not going to eat you."

He tried to smile. "I'm not miserable."

"Well, you shouldn't be. All I'm asking you to do is walk with me. Is there anything wrong with that?"

"Of course not," he said. "I didn't say there was."

"Then why do you keep looking around to see if anyone is watching us? Are you ashamed to be walking with me?"

"No," he said defensively.

She laughed, showing her small, white teeth. "I was just teasing you. I know you're bashful. But any boy as good-looking as you shouldn't be bashful."

Even if he had known where they were going, it would not have mattered. She had disarmed him so completely that he was like a dog at her heels. When they came to the gate in front of her house, she again sensed the rising up of his hesitation. "Amado," she said boldly, "do you think about me?"

He colored and looked away. "Sometimes."

"Do you think about me a lot?"

"I guess so," he said helplessly.

"Amado, do you like me?"

"I can't. You're Tony's girl."

She moved so close to him that he could almost feel her. "I'm not Tony's girl," she said. "I don't belong to anybody. Do you understand that?"

He was so filled with her nearness that he could not have argued if he had wanted to. "I understand," he mumbled.

She tightened her clasp upon his hand. "Amado, let's go inside." She saw the expression in his eyes, and said quickly, "There's nobody home, and there won't be for a long time."

When the door closed behind them, and they were inside, the smothering that Amado had felt in his chest when she clung to him at the snake pen came back to envelop him. She walked away, and he saw the flexing of her rounded hips in the tight skirt.

She turned suddenly and faced him across the room. "Have you ever kissed a girl?"

His voice was shaking. "I don't know."

"I mean it," she said. "I want to know."

He saw that she was deadly serious. "No, I haven't."

When she smiled in relief, he said puzzledly, "Does that make a difference?"

"It makes a lot of difference." She walked across the room to him and slid her arms about his waist. "I'll teach you. It's easy to learn."

When their lips met, he felt his mind reel. She moved closer into his arms, until he could feel her breasts against his chest. They kissed until her lips grew hot under his mouth and her thighs were writhing in agony against his.

When they parted, all her pretense was gone. The eyes that looked up at him were smoky and unreal, and her mouth was drawn down as though it were bared. She took him by the hand into the dim bedroom and closed the door.

As he watched her dumbly, she unbuttoned her blouse. It fell to the floor, and she stood before him with white breasts exposed. They rose and fell with each sharp breath, and she put her hands over them to feel their tautness.

"Please," she moaned when he stood helpless to move. Then, with a flare of anger, she tore at his clothes until he was naked. He was trembling violently. Pulling him down on the bed, she took his hand and put it on her breast. "Here! Hold me here!"

Afterward, Amado could remember little of what happened, except that he had been consumed by a terrible passion and he had clutched at her burning flesh like an animal. Through incoherent spasms of his ecstasy, he heard her cry, "My God! You're hurting me." But he heard her pain and protest as dimly as if they came from another world.

When it was done and he came back to life, and she lay sobbing in rage beside him on the bed, he heard the terrible words that had no meaning for him then but that he would not forget for the rest of his life, no more than if they had been branded on his soul.

# 11

THE CHURCH WAS DARK EXCEPT FOR the red glow of light from the hanging sanctuary lamp. The flame was constant, yet every once in a while it flared wildly from some mysterious rush of air, fighting for its life and throwing desperate gleams in a wide arc toward the ceiling and the spired altar. Finally, it would recover and resume a quiet constancy, and the molten glow would again tumble over the sides of the gold receptacle and onto the lone priest.

It had become a nightly vigil for Father Savio to sit in the darkened church. At the end of the day, when the time of visitants was usually over, he came into the church and turned off the lights and sat down in the first row of seats, almost directly beneath the sanctuary lamp.

At first he had out of habit attempted to pray, but then he had given that up and come only to sit. He could not say that he had come to think, because his mind was not particularly occupied with anything. His rage had spent itself many days ago, and when that had passed, nothing came to take its place. He simply did not care any more.

He was as detached from the whole affair as an observer. On the Sundays that he had to face the people, he went through the ritual of the Mass without really looking at them. In his heart he despised them for their ignorance and their hypocrisy for even daring to enter the house of God, but this was without emotion, too. Afterward, he had watched from his window the long procession on its way to the snake pen. He saw the lust in the procession's common face, and heard the pagan excitement in its voice, and it was the face and the voice of a Roman holiday. Even the same faces and blood were present in the re-enacting. Only the time and circumstance had changed. Quietly in his own mind he had come to an understanding that this was the way it had always been, and that it would always be. When it came to influencing the ways of man, God, after all, was very futile, and His voice was as it had always been, a lonely cry in the wilderness.

A few days before, Father Savio had had the sure knowledge that the dream of the man in the wheatfield was nearing again. He heard the warning with the little bell note of inner sound that was so familiar to him, but this time it was as if an end of things was coming with the dream.

He was mildly surprised that terror did not accompany the warning. There was no panic, and no need to protect himself with prayer. In fact, he found that he was closing with the dream as he had never done before. In his waking mind he saw the golden wheatfield and its arc of blue sky overhead, felt the impact of the brilliant colors against his senses, and understood that the scene was altogether more beautiful than life.

Then, as in the dream's progression, he noticed that there was a figure in shapeless black standing in the wheatfield.

## 111 §

But though he was unafraid now and could think about the man, there was still no face that he could see or imagine. Admitting this, he retreated from his certainty of the face that the dream would one day reveal to him, and contemplated the man in the wheatfield with a new curiosity.

When Father Savio heard the door of the church open, a frown crossed his brow and disappeared as quickly as it had started. He did not even turn around to see who had come in but continued to sit where he was in the red glow of the hanging sanctuary lamp, unmoving and a little huddled, and almost lifelessly still.

Out of the void in which he was immersed, he heard the dimly approaching footsteps falter and come to a stop. There was the sound of heavy breathing in the silent gloom, and then the footsteps began again, hesitant at first and then rapid, striking like blows against the floor of the church. The footsteps were somehow familiar, but he made no effort to recognize them.

At first the import of what he was seeing in the face that stared down did not register in Father Savio's mind. It was Amado, but not as he had ever seen him. He was completely disheveled, and the servile, inward-looking eyes to which Father Savio had grown so accustomed were stretched wide with a shame that made the priest recoil.

"Father! Please!" The words were torn out of a constricted throat.

There was a moment in the meeting of their eyes when the priest's soul wavered and almost fell away in dispassion. Then, in some depth of himself that he had thought dead forever, he felt a stirring, and without his consent, he stretched a hand toward the young man. Amado collapsed to his knees on the floor.

"Father, confess me."

And there, in the great confessional of the open church, the young man revealed his sin in broken, disjointed words. As the priest listened, he was drawn reluctantly back into the world. Through Amado's words he sensed the orgy of the snake pen, and was led into the suffocation of the bedroom and felt the animal contact of the seduction and, unexplainably, because Amado had said nothing about it, the rejection, too. He had raised the young man in his own mold, and for that the priest knew a jealousy as personal as if he himself had been violated.

When it was over and Father Savio had uttered the words of absolution without really hearing them, Amado raised his cleansed eyes to him tearfully. It was like an adoration. The priest turned away. For that brief moment, he hated the young man for his need as he had never hated anybody in his life.

## 12

THE CHILDREN WERE LED BY LUIGI. They came shyly, bearing their booty in burlap sacks and little boxes. Some of them had walked all the way from the farms, and they were hot and sweaty, with expectant smiles on their faces.

They had hardly crossed the threshold of the garage when Tony met them. He blocked their way angrily. "Where do you think you're going?"

Luigi was the spokesman for the group. The others held back in silence. "We got something for Mr. Calder."

"What've you got?"

Luigi surveyed Tony's face carefully before answering. "None of your business."

Tony took a step forward, but Luigi stood his ground defiantly.

"Get out of here," Tony said.

If it were not for Luigi, the rest of the group would have fled in an instant. But he did not budge, and so neither did they. "We came to see Mr. Calder," Luigi said.

"Get out of here and leave him alone," cried Tony, losing his temper.

Behind him, Smale Calder and Pasquale had come from the back yard into the garage, carrying an axle between them. They set it down on the cement floor. "What's the trouble?" Calder said, squinting his eyes to see after the bright sunlight of the yard.

"Damned kids again," said Tony.

Smale Calder crossed the garage heavily, wiping his hands on a grease rag. He looked over the group. "Is that all you kids do is hunt these days?" he said, but his voice was not hard.

"We got something different this time," Luigi said.

The boys smiled in agreement.

"I don't know how much you think them snakes can eat."

"But we got something different this time," Luigi insisted. At his gesture, one of the boys lifted a gunny sack up and down, thumping it on the floor. There was a noisy squawking inside the sack.

Calder was impressed. "By God, I guess you have got something different. What is it? Chicken?"

The boy shook his head. "Not yet."

"I bet he stole it," said Tony.

The boy's eyes bulged with protest. "I did not steal it," he cried. "She's sick. My mother said I could bring her."

"I got something, too," said the other boy with a sack. He held it open shyly for Smale Calder to see.

Calder peered into the dark folds of the sack. "Well, I'll be damned. It's a rabbit."

"And he's mine," said the boy, looking sharply at Tony. "I raised him myself."

"But what do you want to do this for?" Calder asked.

The boy shrugged. "Well, you said the big snake likes rabbits best of all."

"I didn't mean for you to bring your own pet."

The boy made a dismissing wave. "It don't matter. My father would kill him to eat one day, anyway."

Luigi was feeling outdone. "I got the best of all," he said, tapping the wooden box under his arm.

Calder had been appraising the boy with the rabbit. "What you got?" he asked absently.

In answer, Luigi set the box on the floor and opened the top by the barest crack. Smale Calder kneeled down and craned his neck to look inside. He jumped up so suddenly that Luigi almost fell backward in alarm. The top of the box fell shut.

"What's he got?" cried Tony.

"A rat," Calder said in disgust. "He's got a goddamned rat."

Luigi was struck dumb. He stared at Smale Calder with his mouth open. His friends shied away from him uncomprehendingly.

"Get that thing out of here," said Calder. "Don't you ever bring him back again."

Luigi had been humiliated in front of his companions, and he did not even know why. From his darting glances at them, he saw that they were getting a lot of satisfaction out of it. His face grew white.

"Now, take it easy," said Calder. "I didn't mean anything

against you. It's just that a rat is the meanest thing alive. If I let him in there with them snakes, he would tear them apart."

When his words had no effect, Calder put his hand on the boy's shoulder. Luigi shook it off violently and, picking up his box, ran from the garage.

"Let him go," said Tony. "He's no damned good. All he is is trouble."

"I still didn't mean it against him," Calder said. "He didn't know, and I should've told him before."

Everyone had to admit that this time the lizards gave promise of outdoing themselves. From the moment that Smale Calder, standing just inside the gate to the snake pen, emptied out the sack, their actions were fantastic.

There were three lizards in the sack, and two of them immediately went into a scrambling pinwheel around the third, who stayed in place, popping his eyes to adjust them to the sunlight. The children burst into laughter, and even Smale Calder, who did not particularly like to watch the feeding of the snakes, had to smile.

In contrast to the gyrations of the lizards, the snake pen itself was devoid of movement. The afternoon sun hung broilingly over the yard, and all but a few of the snakes had retreated into their caves. The brute snake in his guardian post apart from the others had been lying with only his head showing when Calder opened the gate to the pen. He had rattled listlessly, and then withdrawn into his cave.

As suddenly as the lizards had formed their pinwheel, they broke it and went scampering off toward the rocks, and the children's laughter was cut off with a single gasp of apprehension. One of them climbed to the crest of a rock and began doing pushups. A snake had been sleeping in an open patch of sand beside the rock, and now he came awake. He stirred imperceptibly, watching in mild interest as the lizard performed his exercises. Then, slowly, he began to gather his coils beneath him. Knowing the speed of the lizard, his preparation was liquid in its slowness. He did not seem to be quite ready when the lizard became aware of his presence and froze at the top of his pushup. The lizard moved quickly in escape, but not quickly enough, because the snake reached him just as he gained the far edge of the rock. The blow upended the lizard, so that his white belly showed. He slid down the face of the rock away from his attacker, scrambling with his long toes for a foothold. Then the venom stiffened him, and he collapsed and rolled the rest of the way to the ground. As if he had been waiting all along, another snake glided out of his hole and claimed the lizard and took him inside.

A boy who was hunkered down beside the pen gave a long shuddering sigh. Smale Calder looked at him. The boy's face was white under his olive skin, but perfectly peaceful.

The other two lizards had sensed danger as soon as they reached the rocks. They could not retreat, however, so they raced in panic from one rock to another, unable to rest because as soon as they did the presence of danger would send them leaping away again. The children watched with mouths agape as one of the lizards went visibly crazy under the strain. In one instant, he was leaping away from the menace that lay hidden in the black holes under the rocks, and in the next, he began to run into the holes and out again, seeking out the death that threatened him. His action was so unexpected that he actually got out of three holes in succession, doing nothing more than setting rattles off wherever he went. Finally, he made the mistake of running back into a hole from which he had just escaped. This time the snake was waiting for him.

The last of the lizards had found a temporary refuge against the fence on the other side of the snake pen. The boy who had brought the lizard begged Smale Calder to chase him back into the rocks. Calder shook his head. "When one of them snakes gets hungry enough, he'll go after him. Until then I'm leaving that lizard be. He's got little enough time to live."

"The chicken, then!" cried his owner, and the others shouted their approval.

Calder regarded the boys doubtfully. They begged him with their eyes, and so he picked up the sack that held the chicken and shook her loose inside the snake pen.

Squawking in outrage, the chicken landed in an ungainly heap. She picked herself up and preened down her ruffled feathers with a great show of dignity. As the boy had said, she was not quite grown. There was a bare patch on her back where a sickness showed.

The brute snake had not eaten in nearly two weeks. Now he showed an interest in the chicken, and his great plated head slid out of the cave. The chicken caught the movement and cocked her head inquiringly. Then, as if she had found something to vent her anger on, she burst into a run, her short wings flapping and beak outstretched.

The brute snake saw her coming and began to withdraw his head uncertainly. But he was not quick enough, and the chicken landed one peck squarely on his nose before he disappeared from view. The brute snake rattled furiously, and the sound was magnified in the rock walls of the cave. He nursed his wound for a moment and then poked his head out of the cave, ready to do battle. But by then the chicken had forgotten him and was hopping disdainfully away.

The children were in hysteria, holding themselves around the middle and rocking with laughter. One of them had tumbled to the ground and was shrieking convulsively.

The chicken's victory, however, was short-lived. By this time, the pen was thoroughly aroused, and a snake with thick coils and a mud-colored pattern on his back came out of the rock maze in attack. The chicken was pecking in the sand. She looked over her shoulder once at the approaching snake, and then went back to her search. The snake coiled deliberately and struck. The chicken squawked once, flapped away a few feet in escape, and then fell stiffly on her side. The mud-colored snake followed her and coiled again, waiting patiently while the chicken died.

The boy who had brought the rabbit now stood up proudly and carried his sack over to Smale Calder. "It's my turn."

"For God's sake," Calder said. "Haven't you had enough for one day?"

The boy had anticipated him. "You promised," he said.

Calder reached down and jerked the sack from the boy's grasp. "All right. Get your guts full. It'll be the last time."

The children's faces could have been one, returning his anger with silence and condemning eyes. Calder reached into the sack and took out the rabbit. It made no protest, but lay like a furry ball, almost hidden in the cup of his big hands. For an instant, Calder almost challenged the steady gaze of the children. Then he turned away from them helplessly and, opening the gate to the snake pen, set the rabbit on the ground.

The children knew what they had been waiting for. They turned their attention away from Smale Calder and, squatting down on the ground, settled themselves for what was to follow.

The brute snake must have known, too, because as soon as the rabbit was in the pen, he began to move out of his cave. He paused long enough to test the air with his black tongue, and then he moved relentlessly toward the rabbit.

He rattled only once, when the rabbit made a tentative little hop in halfhearted escape. At the crackling sound, the rabbit began to tremble violently and, turning to face the brute snake, lay back his ears and sat down.

The brute snake did not strike right away, but lay coiled with his great head waving slightly back and forth, playing hypnotically with his prey.

"Get it over with, you son of a bitch," Calder cried.

As if he had heard and understood, the brute snake faltered slightly in the sideways movement of his head. Then the waving resumed like a challenge.

"I'll show you," Calder said, lunging at the gate to the pen.

But he was too late. As soon as he began to move, the brute snake struck. It was a blow of terrible force, much more than he would have needed to kill. There was a squeal of pain from an unused voice, and then the rabbit began to die. But the brute snake was not paying attention to him any longer. He had struck another coil, and his neck was curved again. Smale Calder had paused at the gate, and the brute snake was watching him.

## 13

PASQUALE WAS THE FIRST TO DISCOVER the carnage that the rats had wreaked in the snake pen. He came early to open the garage and unlock the gasoline pumps, and then he went sleepily into the yard to doze in the sun until Tony would come and put him to work.

He passed the snake pen with only a sideward glance before settling himself comfortably on the wooden bench facing the sun. His head drooped forward on his chest, and he almost went to sleep. But something in the back of his mind was bothering him, and he found that his eyes would not stay closed. Finally, he raised his head and blinked into the rainbow colors of the morning light and tried to recall what it was.

After a while he decided that all was not right in the snake pen, and got up to find out what the trouble was. The sight that met his eyes brought him wide-awake in a hurry.

The white sand of the snake pen was strewn with blood. Here and there, some of the rocks were splashed with crimson. At first, Pasquale was at a loss to know what had happened. Then his searching gaze told him the story.

There were two rats in the pen. The swollen body of one

of them, with the nude tail distended, lay near the cave of the brute snake. But the other rat was still alive. He was crouched against the wire fence on the other side of the pen, nearly hidden behind the mutilated rattlesnake on which he had been feeding. He was watching Pasquale warily, his only movement an occasional lifting of his lips to bare his needled, bloody teeth.

On a little patch of sand in the center of the rock maze lay another snake. He was dead, too, with his back a welter of raw gouges where the flesh had been ripped out. Then, as other snakes began to come out of their holes into the warmth of the sunlight, Pasquale saw that at least two more of them bore wounds, and one was torn so badly that he could scarcely drag his length into the sun.

Pasquale's first impulse was to wake up Smale Calder. When he considered the effect his news might have on Calder, however, he whistled under his breath and decided to go over to the saloon and tell Piumbo instead. Smale Calder could find out for himself, and Pasquale did not want to be around when he did.

Tony had just left his house at the far end of the street when he saw Pasquale going into the saloon. He wondered about it, and then guessed that Pasquale had probably had a bad night and needed an eye opener before the day's work. As he approached the garage, though, he saw that the big doors were standing open. Curious, he crossed the street to the saloon to see why Pasquale had left the garage unattended.

Pasquale was relating something to Piumbo and two old men at the bar when Tony came in. What he was saying must have been interesting, because they were all listening to him. Piumbo, however, looked doubtful.

"I never heard of a rat doing anything like that," he said.

Pasquale shrugged. "If you don't believe me, all you got to do is go see for yourself."

Tony tapped Pasquale ungently on the shoulder. "What the hell you doing, leaving the garage open like that while you're over here drinking."

Instead of feeling guilty, Pasquale looked relieved when he saw Tony. "Because I am not going back for a while this morning. That's why."

"Do you want to get fired? What's the matter with you?"

"Nothing is the matter with me. And I am going to keep it that way by not going back over there for a while this morning."

"Will you for Christ's sake tell me what's the matter?"

Piumbo interrupted wearily. "He says some rats got in there and killed Calder's snakes."

Pasquale held up his hand. "Not all of them," he corrected Piumbo. "I didn't say all of them."

Tony wheeled Pasquale around. "Is that the truth?"

"Of course it's the truth," Pasquale said. "If you don't believe it, go over and see for yourself. But I am not going over."

"Is what you're trying to say that Calder doesn't know about it yet?"

"That's what I'm saying."

"Oh, Jesus," Tony said. He bit his lip in thought. "I better go tell him before he sees it for himself. He'll go crazy."

"That's why I am staying over here for a while."

Piumbo untied his apron. "I want to see this."

Tony turned on him. "Mind your own business."

Piumbo regarded Tony evenly for a moment, and then

decided to ignore him. "You don't own the country," was all that he said.

Tony strode furiously to the door and banged it shut on his way out. He was already across the street and entering the garage by the time Piumbo and the two old men at the bar started to follow in his wake. Left alone inside the saloon, Pasquale changed his mind. He shuffled over to the dusty window and peeked through. A few of the shopkeepers who had noticed the commotion were now hurrying across the street, too. Since the discovery had been his, after all, Pasquale decided that he was the rightful one to explain what had happened. He ran back to the bar, gulped down the rest of his drink, and walked with dignity to the garage.

When Smale Calder finally emerged with Tony from the little house, Pasquale was declaiming to the people about what their eyes had already told them. He broke off when he saw Calder, however, and melted into the group.

Calder's silence was more menacing than if he had been in a rage. Without speaking to anyone, he approached the snake pen and surveyed what had happened. Then, methodically, he went to a corner of the yard where there was a heap of odds and ends of lumber, and selected a club. The people stood aside to make an avenue for him on his way back.

Calder paid no attention to the nearness of the brute snake and the ominous rattling inside his cave. He bent down and picked up the dead rat by his nude tail and hurled him high into the air, over the rim of the pen and the board fence, into the street beyond. Then he wiped his big hand on his trousers and picked up the club again.

While this was going on, the other rat had not even

bothered to stop his gorging on the body of the dead snake. But now, as Calder approached him, he backed up until he was braced against the wire fence. He looked sideways once, at the rock maze, as though calculating his chances of escape, and then seemed to realize he was so stuffed and slow that this time he would certainly meet a painful death there. So he chose to fight it out with the man, whose weapons his instincts did not know.

If he ever knew he had made a mistake, he did not reveal it. He waited crouched on his hindlegs, with front paws dangling in the air, until the first blow fell. Even with half of his life gone, he showed his teeth and dragged himself in attack at Calder. But the next blow ended all that.

Before he went about the task of caring for his maimed snakes, Smale Calder came over to the gate of the snake pen and spoke to those who had been watching. "I don't know who did this," he said quietly. "But I know something else. Ever since I started letting people into this yard, I've had nothing but trouble. From now on, this yard is private property and you're not welcome in it, and that goes for everybody in this town."

# 14

THE PEOPLE OF THE TOWN HAD NEVER liked Smale Calder. This did not mean that they disliked him, but simply that they had never really liked him. He was an outsider living among them, and because of this, he had fallen into the neutral ground that is the lot of the outsider.

With Calder, something else had been added. He had broken the code of behavior that the outsider must observe with the insider. He had not tried to come to any understanding with them, though if he had tried to seek their favor or make friends too soon, they would have rebuffed him and laughed at him secretly. But the gesture would at least have made a bond between them.

Instead, he had ignored them completely. He lived alone and did not bother them in the ways they expected. And now in the matter of the snake pen it was he who had rebuffed them. In some curious way, they had become the outsider and he the insider, and it was like an insult.

He had of course given them service and taken their money, but this was a thing of business and had nothing to do with the other kind of understanding. Garzoni brought this up in

Smale Calder's defense the day after he closed the snake pen, but he was howled down by the others in his restaurant.

"Well, I don't care," said Garzoni, thinking of his own role as a merchant. "A man who gives good service has got some credit coming to him."

"That's pretty fine talk," said the widow Lucca's son. "But you'll think differently when next Sunday comes and this place is as empty as it was before."

"I don't know about other people, but I manage to make a living," said Garzoni.

"What kind of a living?" said the widow Lucca's son. "For the first time in years, we've been able to shake some money out of those tightfisted farmers. Now we are back where we started from."

Though it was not his habit, Della Santa was having lunch in Garzoni's restaurant, too. "We are right back where we started from," he intoned. "For a while I thought there was hope for the town in spite of the way it was being run. But now, there's no hope again."

"Perhaps Manuel Cafferata could do something about it," said Garzoni.

Della Santa regarded him petulantly. "What can he do? He is helpless and we all know it."

The widow Lucca's son grunted in agreement. "To hell with Cafferata," he said bitterly. "We ought to do something about it ourselves. What right has Calder got to hurt all of us this way? This is our town, not his. We took him in, and this is the thanks we get."

"That's true," said Garzoni. "But the snakes are still his property."

"They're not his property!" It was Joe Caneva, who had come into the restaurant in time to hear Garzoni's words. He was dressed in his work clothes, and plainly angry. "One of those snakes came off my farm, so he's my property."

Because the entire affair of the snake pen was alien to him, Giometti had been eating in silence. At Joe Caneva's claim, he put down his fork. "For Christ's sake, will you shut up with your talk about who owns those damned things! I'm trying to eat, you know."

Instead of taking offense, Joe Caneva grinned. "What's the matter, Giometti? Don't you like snakes?"

Trying to avoid an argument, Garzoni said mildly, "I wonder who put the rats in with them."

The widow Lucca's son laughed. "Joe Morelli says that the priest put them inside because he was jealous that more people were going to the snake pen than to Mass."

"That sounds like Joe Morelli, all right," said Della Santa.

"I don't believe the lie about the rats, either," said Giometti, who still had not convinced himself that Smale Calder handled live snakes. "This town is crazy with lies."

"But it's true," said Garzoni. "I was there, and I saw what they did. Who would think that a rat could do something like that to a rattlesnake?"

"They'd better not have killed my snake," said Joe Caneva. "I'm going to go see."

"You will not," said Della Santa firmly. "I know what's in your mind, but it's no duty of yours. This is something that Manuel Cafferata must do as mayor of this town."

At the commanding tone in Della Santa's voice, Joe Caneva paused uncertainly. "Cafferata had better do it, then. Because

I'm telling you that I'm mad, and the rest of the farmers are mad, too. Now we got no reason to come to town on Sundays. And that isn't right."

"Amen," breathed the widow Lucca's son under his breath.

When it came to guessing who had put the rats inside the snake pen, there was not too much doubt that it was Luigi. Ever since the incident he had given the garage a noticeably wide berth. But he neither admitted nor denied the act to anyone.

Waiting one morning until old Annapeta had trudged into town on her daily rounds, Tony went to her tin-can shack. Too late, Luigi saw him coming and tried to squirm past the angry figure blocking the doorway. When his demands met with no answer, Tony tried to shake the truth out of him. Luigi let himself hang limp until Tony was finished, and then he got up off the floor, spit in Tony's face, and ran into the desert.

"Sure, I know he was the one who did it," Smale Calder said. "But I brought it on myself, treating him the way I did when he showed me that rat. He was trying to do a good thing, and he got kicked in the stomach for it."

"The kid is crazy," argued Tony. "He ought to be put away."

"He's not nearly so crazy as people think," said Calder. "He's just cruel like any other kid, and he's got to work it out of himself. His only trouble is that he's got more to work out of himself than most."

Baffled, Tony went to Tosca's house that evening and sat with her on the porch, sorting out his anger. She was sober and withdrawn, but there was really no one else to talk to. "I can't figure him out. He should be mad, and he isn't."

"I think he knows it's not Luigi's fault," she said.

"What do you mean by that? Of course it's his fault."

"But only a little part of it. The big fault is Calder's. He knows it. He's taking the blame on himself."

"You're talking like a fool."

"No, I'm not talking like a fool. Calder brought on his own trouble by being what he is. Anybody who's different from other people makes misery for himself. That's the way things are."

Tony was silent. Without her telling him, he had suspected from the beginning what had happened to her. Now, bitterly, he said, "Why did you have to go and do it? You just couldn't let well enough alone, could you?"

"Don't give me a sermon," she said. "You're not the one who was raped."

Tony looked away from the bruised blackness within her eyes. "I don't know what to say."

"You don't have to say anything," she said. "I've told myself all there is to tell. Amado is miserable and indecent, and he's wicked in the worst way anyone can be wicked. But it's not his fault, either."

"I don't understand you."

"That's what I've been trying to explain," Tosca said. "People like Calder and me can't help ourselves. He breaks the rule in one way, and I do it in another. He tries to stay away from trouble, and I go looking for it. But the end is going to be exactly the same for both of us."

# 15

ALTHOUGH IT WAS MORNING, MANUEL Cafferata was near to dozing in Ricami's barber chair. He was not sleepy, but sitting in a barber chair having his hair trimmed always did this to him. It was a pleasure of his day.

The first hint he had that something unusual was happening was when he chanced to glimpse Joe Morelli's cigar make a gyration from the middle of his mouth to the corner. Then Morelli lowered the girlie magazine onto his lap, folded his hands over it, and stared thoughtfully out the window. Manuel Cafferata turned his head to see who was coming.

Behind him, Ricami made a sound of annoyance and pulled his clippers away quickly. He was about to say something when he noticed that both Cafferata and Morelli were looking out the window, and so he looked, too.

The dapper little figure of Della Santa was approaching the barbershop. Ricami peered at the clock on the wall. "Why is he coming so early?" he said. "It's not his time yet."

"I could tell you, Ricami," said Joe Morelli. "But it would take all the fun out of it."

Before crossing the street, the banker sighed visibly. He stepped down onto the dirt and picked his way across, treading as lightly as possible in the dust. When he reached the other side, he mounted to the sidewalk and stamped his feet delicately to shake the dust from his shoes. Then he cleaned his cane with his handkerchief. The three men in the barbershop watched in fascination.

Della Santa acted as though he were entirely unaware that he was being observed. He stopped on the sidewalk, cocking his head to the right and then to the left, studying the front of Ricami's barbershop. Because of his tinted glasses, the men inside could not see his eyes, but they saw his eyebrows go up in mild shock. Shaking his head sadly, Della Santa moved toward the door.

When he came in, Joe Morelli was absorbed in his girlie magazine and Manuel Cafferata was pretending to be in deep thought. Ricami shrugged and resumed his clipping. In his own turn Della Santa acted as if he did not know anyone in particular was inside. "Ricami, you ought to do something about your barbershop," he said sternly. "Just because the rest of the town is going to ruin is no reason you should let it happen to you."

Ricami grunted without interest. "What am I going to do? You tell me."

"You could paint your shop," said Della Santa, hanging up his hat and cane elaborately on the rack. "You could wash your window."

"Why should I wash my window? As soon as I do, a truck will go by and it will be dusty again."

"It's a matter of pride in your shop. I don't let it happen to my bank. My windows are washed every morning although they will be dusty by night." Della Santa sat down in a chair. "Oh, hello, Manuel," he said. "What a pleasant surprise to see you here."

"It don't make any sense to me," said Ricami. "Everyone knows where my barbershop is. They don't come for the view. They come for a haircut and a shave."

Manuel Cafferata nodded his head and muttered good morning as if he were thinking of more important things. In a way, he was. Though he was aware that Della Santa was trying to aggravate him, he knew also that he spoke a measure of truth. There was once a time when Ricami had taken much pride in his barbershop. But the white paint had long since faded from the front of his shop, and even the paint from the sign on his window had chipped away so badly that the words were barely recognizable. Ricami once had another barber in the shop, but now the chair stood empty and unused. The chrome had not been shined in years, and there was a hole in the seat where the horsehair stuffing showed.

Della Santa pretended to notice Joe Morelli for the first time. "Good morning, Morelli," he said in the patronizing tone he reserved for lessers. "You're looking well."

Morelli lowered his magazine. "I wish I could say the same for you, Della Santa," he said. "Are you having trouble with your stomach again?"

Della Santa had not been having trouble with his stomach lately. He knew that his stomach felt fine, and that Joe Morelli was trying to upset him. Still, he could not resist the suggestive twinge he felt in his stomach. He burped, although he did not have to. Morelli smiled in satisfaction.

The banker knew that he should ignore Joe Morelli if he wanted to preserve his dignity. But he had seen that Morelli was reading a girlie magazine. He decided he should not pass up the opportunity to insult him. "You know, Ricami," he said, addressing himself to the barber. "I've wondered often. Where do barbershops get dirty magazines when nobody else has them?"

Ricami smiled mysteriously. "It's a secret among barbers. I am sworn never to reveal it."

Joe Morelli lowered the magazine too quickly, showing Della Santa that he had been reached in a sensitive place. Della Santa pursed his mouth and hummed untunefully.

Joe Morelli had been caught off balance, and he was angry. He tried to keep the vengefulness out of his voice, but he was not altogether successful. "Hey, Ricami," he said. "What time does Della Santa come in for a shave?"

Without glancing at Della Santa, Ricami said, "Oh, he comes in a little later. After you and Cafferata have finished with yours."

"Why does he do that, Ricami?"

"Because he is a banker, and bankers go to work after everybody else."

"Yes, that's true. But is there any other reason?"

"Maybe because he don't like you, too."

"Well then, why do you think he came early today?"

"I don't know," said Ricami, pausing to think. "Maybe he has got something on his mind."

Manuel Cafferata frowned at Joe Morelli in disapproval.

Morelli and Ricami were talking as if Della Santa were not even present. At first the banker had been startled. Then his face took on a dark flush.

"I'm here, you know," he said before he could stop himself.

Ricami regarded him seriously. He turned to Joe Morelli. "That's right. He is here." Then the joke came home to him, and he threw back his head and laughed. "That's a good one, all right."

"You are very funny, Morelli," said Della Santa. "But I can't find it in me right now to laugh. I promise you, though, that there will be a day when I will laugh, not on your jokes, but on your account." He stood up and took down his hat and cane.

"Morelli is right about one thing," he said to Manuel Cafferata. "I have got something on my mind. The people have something on their mind, too, and I speak for them. What this man Calder has done in forbidding the people to come to his snake pen is hurting the business of the town. Ask Ricami. He has had to keep his barbershop open every Sunday because of all the farmers who were coming. Ask Garzoni what has happened to the business in his restaurant. Ask anybody else and you will find out how the town is being hurt."

"Don't forget yourself, Della Santa," said Joe Morelli. "More money in the town means more money in your bank. Don't forget that."

"I'm not forgetting myself," said Della Santa, "because I am a businessman, too. But when there is money in the bank, there is money for the people when they need to borrow it. Those farmers were taking out the money they had buried in the ground, where it wasn't doing anybody any good, and spending it in the town, where it was doing everybody good. Now that is all finished and done with. If you were a good mayor, you would do something."

"What do you want me to do?" demanded Cafferata. "I went to talk to him. He told me to get out. He said he would turn his snakes loose in the desert before he would go through what he has already gone through. Della Santa, you don't know this man. When he says a thing, he means it. He wants to be left alone. Can't you understand that it's done, and nothing is going to change that now?"

Della Santa did not know that Cafferata had gone to see Smale Calder. He was silent for a moment, and then he said, "Calder doesn't have the right to do this thing. He should be taught a lesson. Besides," he added, "all those snakes are not his property. Some of them belong to the people."

"Well, let them come and get their property, then," said Joe Morelli.

Ricami laughed out loud, and even Cafferata grinned. Della Santa opened the door in cold disdain. "As always, Manuel," he said, "it is hopeless to talk to you. I have no other choice but to tell the people that you have failed again."

"When you do," said Cafferata, his voice rising, "remind them that a few months ago you wanted me to make Calder close up his snake pen."

Della Santa regarded Cafferata as though he were a fool. "That has nothing to do with it. The situation has changed."

When Della Santa had gone, closing the door behind him loftily, Cafferata sighed. "Why do you have to make me so much trouble, Joe Morelli?"

"How do I make you trouble? Did you think he came in here to pass the time of day? I tried to save you trouble." He slumped down in his chair and sulked, biting down hard on his cigar.

Because he had rarely seen Morelli lose his temper, Ricami stared at him in surprise. For a moment he was tempted to add fuel to the argument, then thought better of it. He had enough to relate to his customers for a few days anyway. He levered the barber chair back until Manuel Cafferata was in a reclining position.

When his face was wrapped in the steaming towel, Cafferata felt a sense of relief, as though the outside world had for a while been shut off from him.

He could not get out of his mind what Della Santa had said before leaving. What had gone before had nothing to do with his attitude now. The situation had changed. And Della Santa had not been play-acting. He meant every word of it.

Where, then, was the truth of the matter? Or did truth have anything to do with the game that Della Santa and he were playing with each other? Asking this of himself, Manuel Cafferata believed that it did. But as far as Della Santa was concerned, it obviously did not. In saying what he did, Della Santa had revealed the working of his mind in an important way. But at the same time he had revealed Cafferata to himself, and thereby posed the inscrutable thing that had been happening to him ever since the coming of the snake pen.

As he had found himself doing so often lately, Father Savio turned away uncomfortably from the unvoiced question burning in Amado's eyes. After the morning Mass the priest finished with his unvesting as quickly as he could and then tried to beat a retreat from the sacristy. But Amado was not to be put off. He had followed doggedly on the heels of the priest until they were outside the church, and was holding him there in conversation.

Amado had changed, and he was continuing to change every day with the fanatic determination of one who has been redeemed. Father Savio was not unfamiliar with the emotion. He had seen it often enough in seminary, but there he had accepted it as merely another shading in the vocation that possessed them all in one form or another. Once he had heard an old priest say in an unguarded moment, "Spare me from the redeemed." Father Savio had thought the remark sacrilegious and had put it out of his mind, but now it came back with a different meaning.

Father Savio rubbed his hands together and forced himself to smile affably. "Well, Amado, I guess it's time you were getting on to your job."

"I don't care about that any more," Amado said. "It's not important to me."

"Still, you have an obligation to your duty."

"My duty lies higher now," said Amado stubbornly.

Father Savio groaned within himself. "Yes, I know," he said. "And we must be thankful that soon you are going to fulfill that duty. But until then you shouldn't neglect . . ."

"Father, please," Amado interrupted, "there's something I have to talk to you about."

So there it was, the first broaching of the question the priest did not want to hear, but that he could not escape any longer.

"All right, Amado," he said. "I guess we can talk about it over breakfast."

As they made their way to the house, Father Savio was resentful. He had permitted himself to be drawn back into life by Amado's need, and the return was a reluctant one. He could remind himself that to feel this way was wrong because he had been of no use to God in the depths of surrender into which he had been plunged. Nevertheless, it had been a seclusion of unthinking and unfeeling peace, the peace of utter surrender, and in a curious way he had enjoyed it.

They ate their breakfast beneath the hovering presence of Mrs. Ricco, who paused five times if she stopped once to plant a kiss on Amado's head and hurl unsubtle challenges at Father Savio that vocation had come to her son, as she had predicted all along. Father Savio did not respond, but heard her out calmly, so much so that once he caught himself wondering bemusedly what her reaction would be if he told her that Amado had found his vocation in a bedroom.

Father Savio shook his head to be rid of the thought. He, too, had changed, in the tortured way of his return, and this was the real reason he could not cope with Amado's passion. Once, and it seemed such a long time ago, he could have embraced the boy's vocation with open arms, and probably even fired it higher. But now he could not rise to it. He felt a spectator as detached from life as when he had been a child and very sick and had watched the light make patterns on the curtains in his room.

Father Savio felt Amado's eyes upon him and looked up in time to see accusation there. *So he knows, too, that I have changed*, the priest thought, but it did not bother him. He met Amado's gaze and said, "What was it you wanted to speak to me about?"

Because he had been caught in an unguarded moment, there was a fleeting return of boyish embarrassment in Amado's revealing eyes. It faded quickly, though, and his tone as he spoke to the priest was that of an equal. "I know you don't like to talk about this any more, Father," he said. "If you would rather, I won't do it."

"No, please go ahead," said Father Savio, observing to himself that the understanding between them was so sure that Amado had neglected to mention what it was he wanted to talk about.

"I don't know if you've heard, but Smale Calder has closed up the snake pen to the people. He won't let anybody in to see his snakes any more."

"Yes, I've heard that," said Father Savio.

Amado's brows were knit in confusion. When he realized that Father Savio was not going to say anything more, he began to flounder through an explanation of the talk he had heard in the store. "From what everyone says, Calder isn't fooling. He even told Manuel Cafferata that he would rather turn the snakes loose in the desert than let the people see them any more."

"Yes, I heard that, too," said Father Savio. "Della Santa came by to tell me."

Amado regarded the silent priest with growing bafflement. "But I don't understand. It doesn't make sense to me."

Unable to meet Amado's eyes, Father Savio looked down at the table. "What doesn't make sense to you, Amado?"

"There must be a reason why he's doing this. He came to this town to work his evil on the people, to turn them away from God. And now he isn't doing it any more."

"Perhaps there is a reason that we don't understand," Father Savio said lamely.

"But you said yourself that the serpents were his handmaids in arousing the people to lust," Amado burst out. "Are you forgetting that, Father?"

If no one else had listened, at least Amado had listened, and well, Father Savio remarked. So much so that the repeating of his own words fell upon the priest's ears with an import that frightened him.

"You are forgetting what he did to me," cried Amado. "You're forgetting that I am suffering from the evil he did to me."

Father Savio regarded Amado in amazement. It was the first time that the other face of righteousness had been made clear to him. In the sorting of Amado's conscience, the young man had absolved himself of all guilt in what he had done. He had placed the blame for his fall into sin squarely on Smale Calder's shoulders, and the priest could say nothing because he himself had set this reasoning into motion. *How very convenient,* the priest thought, *and how very dishonest.*

"I'm not forgetting that," said Father Savio in a tone of guilt that was unexplainable to himself.

"Then why is he doing this?" pleaded Amado.

"I don't know," Father Savio said slowly. "I don't know the answer any more."

## 16

THE BOY WHO HAD BEEN STATIONED AT the fence made a low sound, and the others turned their heads to look at him. They watched him straighten up and then bend down again and press his face to the fence. After a moment he joined them where they were sitting in the deeper darkness of the bushes.

"All right, he's gone to bed," the boy said. "Let's go."

Luigi got to his feet. When the others began to follow suit, he waved them back down again. "Wait a minute," he said in a harsh whisper. "Let me see for myself." He tiptoed quietly to the fence and, screwing his face to the crack, surveyed the yard. Smale Calder's light had gone out, and the house was dark. Before he backed away, Luigi took a look at the snake pen. The rocks were bathed in pale light from the rising moon. He looked at the cave where the brute snake lived, set apart from the rest, and thought he saw a movement. Luigi went back to the clearing in the bushes and sat down.

"Let's go," said the boy who had been stationed at the fence.

"Shut up," snapped Luigi. "How do we know he's asleep yet?"

"What's the matter?" the boy said sarcastically. "Are you backing out?"

"If you're so brave, why don't you do it?" said Luigi.

"I'm not the one who said I could."

"Shhh," whispered another boy. "Someone's coming."

They huddled closer together in the concealment of the bushes and fell quiet. There was a slow sound of footsteps in the street, and then a bent figure in black detached itself from the shadows and moved into the clearing of moonlight. It was old Annapeta, going home with her sack of pickings slung over her shoulder.

"It's only your mother," whispered the boy who had been taunting Luigi.

"She's not my mother," said Luigi. "My mother is dead."

"Then why do you live with her?" said the boy.

"Shut up," said Luigi.

"If she's not your mother, can I throw a rock at her?"

"Leave him alone," another boy whispered.

"Go ahead and throw a rock at her," said Luigi. "But if you hit her and she yells, then we're finished for the night."

This seemed to make sense to the boy. He snickered, but he was quiet.

Annapeta had nearly crossed the clearing of moonlight when she paused. Her shawled head turned in the direction of the bushes, and the moonlight played on her emaciated white face. Luigi felt the boy next to him shiver. They waited, hardly daring to breathe, until Annapeta finally resumed her journey, shuffling into the shadows.

When they could hear her footsteps no longer, they stood up to ease their cramped legs. "I bet she heard us," one of the boys said.

"So what," Luigi said in a strained voice. "She won't say anything." He cleared the longing in his throat and moved suddenly to the fence. "Let's go."

Two of the boys made a stirrup with their hands and boosted Luigi to the top of the fence. He looked to see where he would land, and then climbed down the brace boards on the other side. Waiting until the last of the three had been pulled up, he made his way silently to the snake pen. By the time the others joined him, he was fumbling at the latch to the gate.

A rustling sound so slight that it might have come from the wind in the trees brought all of them up stock-still. Luigi stared into the snake pen and saw the beginnings of movement in the rocks. It was like shadows moving within shadows. He swallowed audibly, and the others heard him.

"I don't know," whispered one of the boys uncertainly. "Do you think you can do it?"

Luigi hesitated, drawing his hand away from the latch, and then his glance fell on the dark outline of Smale Calder's house. His mouth curled contemptuously. "Sure I can do it," he said out loud. "It's just a trick." He leaned forward and jerked open the gate.

"You don't have to, you know." It was the boy who had taunted him earlier. But now there was a quaver in his voice.

"I said I could, didn't I?" Luigi threw back over his shoulder. He pulled the gate shut behind him and stepped into the snake pen. He faltered only once, when a flurry of warning rattles met the sound of his first step, and then he moved defiantly to the center of the patch of sand. In the moonlight his head with its mass of tight blond curls shimmered like a crown.

Luigi went down on his knees in the sand and began a low chanting singsong, as he had heard Smale Calder do. The whirring bursts of rattles in the labyrinth of rocks grew louder. Sweat beaded out on Luigi's brow until his face was shining wet, but still he went on with his singsong. Incredibly, the rattling seemed to grow quieter, and then it subsided altogether. There was movement everywhere in the rocks. A dark curving shape moved out of the shadows onto the patch of sand. Another followed it, and then another.

The brute snake, however, was the first to reach Luigi. When his great golden coils began to slide out of the den, the boys saw it, but Luigi did not. They clung together in terror, and one of them tried to call out to Luigi, but the only sound that came out of his throat was a croak.

When Luigi finally saw the brute snake, it was only a few feet away from him. He started, but so slightly that the movement was almost imperceptible. The brute snake stopped and methodically gathered his coils beneath him, but he did not rattle. His great head hooked back, but he did not strike. He seemed simply to be watching the boy.

The liquid motion in the snake pen flowed to a stop. Luigi had become as still as a statue, his hands resting in his lap and his head inclined in the direction of the brute snake, so that he had the appearance of one hypnotized. Now he was almost completely surrounded by the other snakes, but he was unaware of them. All his attention was on the brute snake.

Luigi was the first to move. As if it were a disjointed

member, one of his hands raised up slowly and with palm outward began to ease toward the brute snake. He nearly succeeded. His hand was only inches away from the mass of golden coils when the brute snake lowered his head, as if withdrawing from the boy's touch. The movement was so sudden that Luigi jerked back his hand.

Luigi made only one sound. It was when the brute snake's fangs had sunk and fastened into the flesh of his hand, and it was like the cry of a child who is lost. He scrambled to his feet with the brute snake still hanging to him, and turned in the direction of the gate. Before he could take a single step, the snakes who had been gathered around struck furiously at his bare legs. He cast one wild look at the others outside the snake pen, and then he crumbled to the ground.

The boy who had taunted Luigi was the first to reach the fence. He was older than the others, and wiser, too, and before they climbed over, he shook into each one of them a warning that terrified them. They scattered in the darkness and did not stop running until they had gained the safety of their beds.

Smale Calder came wide-awake at dawn with the knowledge that something had gone wrong. He lay in bed with his eyes open and tried to piece together his disquiet. He thought he could remember hearing sounds in the night and trying to rouse himself to find out what they were. Then the sounds had stilled, and he had fallen again into a drugged sleep.

He remembered something else, but he was not certain whether he had dreamed it or not. Much later in the night there had been a persistent knocking at his door, like the beat of a drum. Again, he had tried to rouse himself, but then the knocking had stopped. He had lifted himself up on an elbow and looked out the window, and through blurred eyes imagined he had seen the figure of a woman in black standing beside the snake pen. He remembered deciding then that it was a dream, and had relaxed back onto the bed. Now he was not quite sure.

Lying in bed, he gazed out the window and saw the first sunlight filtering through the leaves of the cottonwood tree. His lids grew heavy and he closed his eyes. Then suddenly he remembered what the sounds were that he had heard in the night, and sat upright. They had been the warning sounds of rattlesnakes. And what had wakened him later was not a dream after all. The figure in black had been old Annapeta.

When Tony came to work, he found Smale Calder sitting on the bench in the yard with his face buried in his hands. He did not look up when Tony said his name. Tony stood beside him uncertainly, knowing that something had happened but unable to comprehend what it was. Instinctively, he turned to the snake pen.

Luigi lay huddled on the patch of sand. His knees were drawn up and his arms were locked over his face, like a child who had gone to sleep in the warm sunlight. But anything resembling a child, or a human being, for that matter, ended there. The little body was swollen so grotesquely that if it had not been for the unmistakable tangle of blond curls, Tony would not even have known who it was. He leaned weakly against the cold stone of the garage.

Smale Calder did not move even when Pasquale clumped noisily through the garage and came into the yard muttering apologies for being late. Pasquale looked wonderingly at

Calder, and then at Tony, and then at the snake pen. "*Madre mia,*" he murmured. He sidled closer to the pen. "But what is Luigi doing in there?"

Before he could stop himself, Tony laughed out loud. "What do you think he's doing in there, you damned fool?" he cried. "He's dead."

"That's clear to see," Pasquale said. "But what I would like to know is why he is in there."

Tony cursed him until he could think of nothing else to say, and then he felt better. Pasquale heard him out and shrugged and went back to the snake pen. "He shouldn't be left like that," Pasquale said, shaking his head.

Tony moved closer to the bench where Calder sat hunched. "He's right about that. You got to get him out of there." When Calder didn't move, Tony said hesitantly, "It's going to be bad enough when the town finds out. If they see him inside there, it's going to be worse."

Calder raised a haggard face to him. "What do you mean by that?"

Tony was not quite sure what he meant. "I don't know," he said. "I just know." He returned Calder's empty stare helplessly. The face that looked up at him was not any face he had known before. All the man's strength seemed to have washed out of him, and he was haggard and old.

Calder heaved himself slowly to his feet and went to the snake pen. Tony remarked to himself that not one of the snakes who lay basking in the sun made a sound when he entered. Calder stood over the huddled body of the boy for a long time, and then he picked him up as gently as if he were alive and carried him out of the snake pen.

## 149 §

When the boy had been laid on the bench, Tony looked around for something to cover him, and then took off his jacket quickly and covered as much of the ravage as he could. Because he had not had a chance to see all that he wanted to, Pasquale was annoyed and took no pains to hide it.

Smale Calder had turned his back on them and was walking heavily toward the house. Tony watched him for a moment, and then called out in a stricken voice, "It's not your fault that he's dead. Don't you understand that?" But Calder made no sign that he had heard.

## 17

Tony screwed the top on the gasoline tank and tried to appear casual as he asked Joe Caneva what he was doing in town twice in the same day. Joe Caneva pretended to be busy with a stubborn ignition key. "I forgot something," he said, and added with a little more conviction, "I got to go to the saloon for some whisky."

"Well, you can leave your truck here while you go," said Tony. "I'm closing up the garage for the night, anyway."

Joe Caneva was flustered. "No," he said quickly. "I'll take it over to the saloon."

Tony shrugged. "That's up to you. It's only across the street. I thought it would save you the trouble of moving."

"Thank you, Tony. You're a good boy." Caneva stepped on the starter, raised his hand in a short wave, and wheeled the old truck across the street.

Tony watched him go into the saloon. It occurred to him that Joe Caneva had changed into his overalls. That morning, when he had come into town the first time, his family had been with him and he had been wearing good clothes.

Before shutting the door that led from the garage to the yard, Tony thought again about going to see Smale Calder. Calder had not been out of the house all day. Even when the sheriff from the county seat had come to investigate Luigi's death, Calder refused to come out to see him, and the sheriff had to go inside. What they said to each other nobody knew, but it must not have been satisfactory to the sheriff, because he had come out angrier than before.

In the beginning dusk the little house seemed lonely and forsaken. For the first time since he had known Smale Calder, Tony sensed that the man needed someone to talk to, but he did not know what he could say to him that would help. What had happened was so hopelessly final that there seemed nothing really to talk about, except perhaps to lie, and Calder was not a man to listen to lies. Tony retraced his steps to the front of the garage, where Pasquale was leaning against the big sliding door.

Tony fastened the lock that Smale Calder had put on the door when he had barred the town from coming to see the snake pen. There was a slot in the stone where the mortar had fallen away, and Tony pushed the key inside. When he turned, he noticed that Pasquale was watching him with more than a little interest. Tony would not have attached any importance to this except that at that moment another truck pulled up across the street. Now the front of the saloon was lined with trucks from the farms.

"What's going on over there, Pasquale?"

There was a pause before Pasquale answered. "How should I know?"

"Because you've been over there at least six times today."

"That don't mean nothing," said Pasquale. It was nearly dark and Tony could not see his face, but Pasquale shifted uncomfortably. "Well, I'll see you tomorrow." He walked away.

"Wait a minute," Tony called. "I want to talk to you."

Pasquale quickened his pace. "I'll see you tomorrow," he said over his shoulder.

Tony was tempted to follow him to the saloon. But for some reason he could not put his finger on, he knew that his presence would not be welcome there this night. As he stood undecided in the darkness, he saw the burly figure of Giometti go into the saloon and slam the door shut behind him. A moment later, he saw Garzoni leave his restaurant and, looking to right and left, hurry into the saloon.

Tony had a sudden thought. He turned on his heel and walked quickly up the back street toward Tosca Morelli's house. Leaving the gate unlatched, he bounded up the steps to the porch and knocked. When Tosca opened it and saw him, her eyes widened in alarm.

"Is your father here?"

"No, he isn't. He's with Manuel Cafferata." Her gaze played over Tony's grim face and troubled eyes. "You're beautiful," she said.

"Don't," he said. "Something's going on and I have to find out what it is. Are you sure your father is with Manuel Cafferata?"

"I was just there to ask him if he was coming home for dinner. What's the matter?"

"I don't know. I got to find out what it is."

Tosca stepped onto the porch. "I knew something was happening all day."

Tony had been about to leave. He turned back. "What do you mean by that?"

Tosca shrugged. "I'm not sure exactly," she said. "But when Della Santa took Luigi's body to his house, I went to see him."

"Good God. What did you do that for?"

"Because I wanted to see him," Tosca flared. "That's why."

"All right, all right," said Tony placatingly. "What went on there?"

Tosca regarded him with impatience, and then she said, "You know everybody was coming to see Luigi before the sheriff took his body. I stayed for a while, and I noticed that Della Santa was asking some of the men outside to talk to them. I sneaked up to hear what he was saying, but when he saw me, he quit talking until I went away."

"That means there's going to be trouble," said Tony. "Did Della Santa talk to your father?"

"Don't be foolish."

Tony was about to say that he was not being as foolish as she thought. Instead, he touched her arm gently in good-bye. "I'll bet your father knows, though. And I'll bet Manuel Cafferata knows." What he did not say was that if they did know, what were they doing in Manuel Cafferata's office when everyone else was at the saloon?

At his touch, Tosca shivered. "Please don't leave me. I need you tonight."

"I've got to go," cried Tony. "Don't you see that whatever they're planning, it has to do with Calder?"

When she saw that she could not hold him, she flung his hand away. "I hope it does," she said. "Ever since he came to this town, you've been somebody else."

Tony left her crying on the porch. She was wrong about that. It had come to him with crystal clearness that he was more himself than he had ever been.

# 18

THE LAST OF THE DARK FORMS HAD passed, and the street outside Manuel Cafferata's window was still. Because he had been involved with each of them in an important way from the beginning, their passage had been like pages closing in a book. It was curious how you remembered a man for one thing alone, even though you had been involved with him in a hundred things, and the one thing you remembered him for usually had to do with a time of trouble.

He was disturbed that friendship had so little to do with the remembering. There was not one man of them he could truthfully call a friend. Rather, it had been like a procession of favors conferred, and the favors had to do with the practical business of living instead of matters of the heart. The way that each man had passed showed at last how the favors had been received. The little men had passed with defiance, and the good men, remembering the involvement that the lighted window meant, had passed with regret.

But how they had passed did not mean much to him now. What mattered was the fact that they were convinced they had no other choice. They had taken the affair of the snake pen into their own hands, and he had nothing to do with it any more. When the last of them was gone from sight, Manuel Cafferata finally knew that time itself had passed him by.

He was seeing things very clearly. Tomorrow he would not, because he could feel the stirrings of self-pity and recognize them for what they were, and a deeper stirring of the hatred that would consume him after that. He wondered how long it would take to know the peace of final resignation, or if he ever would.

Now that it had happened, he felt no surprise at all, because he remembered that it had begun to happen long ago. He had turned that corner when everything he did seemed to be wrong. Before he turned that corner, he could have done the same things and been right, because they had chanced to happen in the right time. But after he had turned the corner, he could have been Christ on earth and still be wrong, because it was in the wrong time.

Once he could have stepped down and been respected, and probably a little loved. Knowing this, what was it in a man that forced him to go on outside his time, when he could see that only defeat and humiliation lay in front of him.

When he had awakened that morning and heard the news of Luigi's death, he had felt a pang, as of the final stab of a pain that had grown old and familiar. He had known then that it was all over. The sheriff from the county seat hardly had to say what he did, in Smale Calder's yard, in plain sight and hearing of everyone. "You are one hell of a mayor, or whatever it is you're supposed to be, to let a thing like this happen."

Cafferata had tried to explain something about private property. The sheriff had looked at him incredulously and said, "It's the first time I've heard of rattlesnakes being private property." Then he had gone in and accosted Smale Calder in his house and come out with the angry and threatening expression of a baffled bull. That at least had given Cafferata some satisfaction, but it was short-lived, because the sheriff had said, "Whether anyone likes it or not, I'm going to keep an eye on things around here from now on." And Della Santa had moved quickly into the breach and said, looking significantly at those around him, "That won't be necessary. Not at all. We will take care of this affair ourselves."

Cafferata suddenly felt tired. He was overcome with an infinite weariness, and all he wanted to do was go to bed. The presence of Joe Morelli, who sat with nothing to say because he, too, realized that it was the end of things as far as Manuel Cafferata was concerned, was uncomfortable to him.

"You ought to go get a drink, Joe Morelli."

Morelli knew what he meant, and for an instant the mask that had been settling all day on his big face relaxed. "I don't want to go down there," he said. "What they're going to do is no interest to me."

"Afterward, they will remember that you weren't there."

Joe Morelli dropped his eyes to conceal his astonishment. When it came to an understanding of the way things actually worked in life, Cafferata was at times almost childish. He was a leader, or at least he once had been, but he was blind to people. "What do I care what they think?" he said, relieved to make a show of nobility.

"Della Santa will remember you weren't there. You

shouldn't make more of an enemy out of him than you have already."

It was as close to voicing surrender as Cafferata could come. Joe Morelli winced. "Let him remember," he said, but this time he could not pretend to be noble. He knew that whatever he had said or done to Della Santa in the past meant nothing. When the time came, he would make peace with Della Santa because he needed him, and Della Santa would accept it, if for no other reason than to keep an eye on him.

Joe Morelli felt impelled to voice part of this knowledge at the risk of revealing himself. "Della Santa won't bother me," he said. "Nor you, either, Manuel."

"Why do you say that? You know how he feels about me."

Joe Morelli wanted to say, *Because you are out of the way. Can't you see that? Really, he will treat you good, and you'll be gratified and even begin to think you were wrong about him, when the truth is that he never had anything against you for yourself, but only your position.*

Instead, Joe Morelli said, "Because of all you have done for this town. Why, you got to remember, Manuel, that there wouldn't even be a town here if it wasn't for you."

"People don't remember that," said Cafferata morosely. "Nobody remembers that."

"Maybe not right now," said Joe Morelli. "But afterward, they will."

"I hope," said Cafferata. "I hope they do remember that." He was silent for a moment. "When I think of all the years," he murmured.

Joe Morelli could see that his words had helped Cafferata, but also that he was beginning to feel sorry for himself. This

Joe Morelli did not want to see, at least now. He stood up abruptly. "You better go to bed, Manuel," he said. "You look tired."

Cafferata had just begun to feel better. But when he thought about it, he remembered that he had been very weary. "I guess you're right. I am tired." He smiled sentimentally at Morelli, and said without malice, "Good night, Joe. I still think you ought to go get a drink."

Joe Morelli managed a gruff good night and went out quickly. When he was in the darkness, he gave an immense sigh of relief. It was hard enough to do what he had to do, without having to see Cafferata like that. To be witness to any man in his death throes was something that he had never been able to abide, because he believed that this kind of death was senseless.

*Life after all,* thought Joe Morelli, *is a question of recognizing your enemy.* That was simple enough, though some people out of weakness or high thoughts could never admit to themselves that there was an enemy. After that, it was a question of how you met your enemy. Because they knew themselves to be strong, men like Cafferata chose to meet their enemy with strength. But in such a contest, there was always a victor and a vanquished, and this time Cafferata was the vanquished.

The wiser route was to come to terms with your enemy. In this way a man was never the loser, and what was most important, he could keep on living. *I am the real immortal,* thought Joe Morelli. *Things begin with men like Cafferata, and they end with me.* It was a comforting thought, but mingled with it was the remembering of an old man alone, a strong man who had been clearly vanquished. For a brief moment Joe Morelli was not very content with himself.

When he had left Cafferata's office, Joe Morelli really had no intention of going to the saloon. But when he turned down the street that led to his house, he saw Tony approaching. He caught one glimpse of the boy's determined face and abruptly turned on his heel. *Oh Christ, here comes another one.* He ignored the young man's calling his name, and hurried in the direction of the saloon. He would have a drink after all, but that would be the end of it. He would have nothing to do with their dirty business.

When he saw that Manuel Cafferata's office was dark, a panic began to seize Tony. His mind was spinning from the craziness of things. It was like a dream in which many figures moved mysteriously, and he was clamoring to be heard, but nobody could see him or hear him. He pounded on the door, not even sure that Cafferata was inside, except that there had been something about Joe Morelli's manner that told him he was. A pale light showed through the window, and Tony felt a settling within himself.

Manuel Cafferata was like a stranger. His expression was startled and even fearful, as though he had anticipated danger at his door. "Oh, it's you," he said. He stood listening for sounds. "Come inside."

Cafferata moved to pull the string to the big bulb that hung from the ceiling, and then changed his mind and turned to face Tony in the dim light from the room beyond. Tony saw that he had been getting ready for bed. Without his coat and vest, Cafferata looked old and defenseless.

§

"What do you want?" Cafferata said in an empty voice.

Tony almost groaned with the returning unreality. He knew that something of menace was going on in the town. Even the air seemed filled with it. Yet, here was Cafferata going to bed as if nothing were happening. Suddenly, Tony was convinced that he had imagined it all, that there was no conspiracy of silence, that everyone was acting normally, because all was as it should be. He stared foolishly at Cafferata.

A quizzical interest showed in Cafferata's face. "Why, you don't know," he said. "But of course they wouldn't have told you, either."

Tony's mind reeled again with the confirmation, and he put out his hand for support. Cafferata caught his elbow to steady him. "You better go home," he said.

Tony heard his own voice as a child's. "What are they going to do?"

"Nothing that is your affair," said Cafferata. "Go home, or you will make yourself a trouble you'll be sorry for."

Tony pulled his arm free. "Will you tell me what they're going to do!"

Cafferata had begun to come out of himself. Now he shrugged in dismissal. "What is it to me," he said. "They are going to destroy the snake pen."

If Cafferata had said the men of the town were going to horsewhip Smale Calder, Tony could have accepted it easier. "They can't," he said, looking at Cafferata with a building horror. "They don't know what they're doing."

"You are wrong there," said Cafferata. "Maybe not in their heads, but they know in their hearts. They say they are protecting the town, but what they are really doing is getting even with Calder. And," he added bitterly, "they are getting even with me."

"But it's more than that," cried Tony. "Don't you understand it's a lot more than that?"

"What more than that? What more than killing a bunch of snakes for an excuse."

Suddenly, Tony was shouting to break through Cafferata's comprehension. "But they're not only snakes! Don't you see if they kill the snakes, they are killing him, too!"

"I don't know what you're talking about," said Cafferata. But even as he said it, he remembered that he once had known, but that now he did not. At Tony's words, the impenetrable barrier had risen up in front of him again, and at last he realized that it concealed the secret of his own undoing. A weariness like death came over him, and he turned away, leaving the young man standing in the darkened room.

"You could do something about it if you wanted to," Tony cried after him accusingly.

*Now, it's you who don't understand,* said Cafferata to himself. *You are a young man and I am an old man, and it is foolish for us to talk, because we don't speak the same language.* Aloud he said, "It's none of my affair. It's too late for that."

There was a hollow roar in the night. It was an explosion without substance, like the opening of a furnace door. Cafferata wheeled in the entrance to his bedroom. The young man's face was twisted with pain. Then he turned and ran like a madman into the night.

# 19

FATHER SAVIO HAD BEEN SO CERTAIN the idea was preposterous, that Smale Calder would actually come at his beckoning, that he had consented to it only to please Della Santa. Now, in the stillness, the creaking of the gate, opening once and then unmistakably opening wider to admit another person, was shrill as a scream. Father Savio's heart constricted with fright.

He heard the sound of footsteps on the stone walk that led to the kitchen door, and it was like the approaching drumbeat of all the terrors he had known in his life. The confrontation was at hand, and he was not prepared for it. In his mind he saw Smale Calder as he had first seen him, a shapeless figure emerging from the gloom of the garage into the sunlight. He felt the animal revulsion that the incident in the street had provoked in him. He remembered the despair and absolute surrender of his rejection by the people. And wound through everything that tumbled into his remembering, inexplicably, was the faceless dream of the man in the wheatfield.

There was a knocking at the door, but he was powerless to move. There was a silence, and then he heard Amado call his name. The sound of the voice was reassuring, and Father Savio leaped at the possibility that Calder was not with him after all. But even as he thought it, he knew it was not true, because he could actually feel the man's palpable presence. When the knock came again, he gathered his numbed wits with a desperate effort of will and took a faltering step toward the door. Before he reached it, the door opened and Amado's thin face was framed in the light. "Father?" he called, and then he saw the priest. There was only puzzled inquiry in the word. That and the absence of fear in the young man's face brought Father Savio to his senses. "I'm sorry. Please come in," he heard himself saying in a normal voice.

Amado stepped aside, and Smale Calder's huge bulk filled the door. He came uncertainly into the kitchen, his head bent as if making sure of his footing before anything else. An awareness that the man was clumsy went absurdly through Father Savio's mind. But when Calder looked up, Father Savio took in his breath sharply. There was nothing clumsy about his eyes. The man had a force. About that the priest had not been mistaken. But in the brief instant before Father Savio turned away he was astounded to realize that it did not clearly contain the evil he had expected.

Still, he could not be sure, and when he heard Amado excusing himself, there was a quick return of terror that he was being left alone with Calder. He was at the point of asking Amado to stay when he saw the young man's triumphant smile. Immediately, Father Savio remembered the purpose of sending for Smale Calder. He frowned in distaste. When

Amado went out the door, his mouth was caught up in a thin line.

Without meeting Calder's gaze, Father Savio said, "There are easier chairs in the next room. Would you like to talk in there?"

Smale Calder's voice was almost uncaring in its emptiness. "I'm not a man for comfort, if you don't mind."

As much as anything else, Father Savio had wanted to escape the harsh, revealing light of the kitchen. "I don't mind," he said. "We can sit in here." He went to the cupboard. "I can give you a glass of wine. It's not blessed yet," he said with a forced laugh, "so you don't have to worry that we'll be drinking sacramental wine."

"Well, I don't usually," said Calder. "But I guess I could stand some tonight."

When they had sat down under the glare of the naked bulb that hung from the ceiling, Father Savio pretended to be occupied with an inner thought so that he would not have to look at Smale Calder. For no reason that he could explain, he remembered an experiment he had once wanted to conduct in seminary. Believing that every man lived a pose in life and that words were only a concealment behind which he lived, Father Savio had wanted to put two people who did not know each other into a room. No words were to be spoken between them. They were to sit at a table and stare into each other's eyes. When they were done, he believed, each would know the other's true soul more surely than words could ever reveal.

Yet now, confronted by the very man whom he had judged without knowing him and whose soul he most wanted to see, Father Savio found that he could not meet his eyes. Curiously, it was not only that he feared what he would find in Smale Calder's eyes, but also that he feared what Calder would find in his.

"We don't know each other, Mr. Calder," he said, fixing his attention studiously on the wine glass in front of him. He waited an instant for Calder to speak, but when he did not, he realized he had not said anything that deserved an answer. "Since you came to this town, you have avoided me," he began again. Then, knowing that this was not the whole truth, he added quickly, "And I have avoided you. Are you wondering why I asked you to come here tonight?"

"I am," said Calder, "though I think I know, and I appreciate it. A man don't like to be alone too long when he knows a boy's death is on his hands."

Father Savio did not know what he expected to hear, but he had not expected this. Despite himself, he tore his gaze from the table and looked at Smale Calder. There was an unmistakable sadness in the man's eyes. In disbelief, Father Savio heard himself saying with sympathy, "But what happened today was not your fault."

"Oh, it was my fault, all right, and I've got to admit that. If I didn't have them snakes, that boy would be alive today."

"You didn't kill the boy," Father Savio protested. "The snakes did." Then, struck with a thought he knew to be true, he said, "And the boy killed himself, too. He was looking for death."

What the priest said passed across Smale Calder's brow without comprehension. "What it comes down to is this, Father." He said the unused word tentatively and, seeming not to dislike it, went on, "Them snakes are as much a part of me as I am myself. If I can't live without them, then a man like me shouldn't be where there are people around." Calder spoke slowly, looking at nothing now, except within himself, as though he were sorting the decisions that had come to him that day. "Either that, or if I have to stay in a town, I should have made myself live without them, which is why I got to get rid of them now."

Father Savio was startled. "Do you mean you're going to destroy them?"

"Lord, no," Calder said angrily. "I couldn't kill them no more than I could kill myself. I'm going to take them out to the desert where they belong, and let them go." His voice quieted, looking inward again to his thinking. "Then someday, when I can afford not to have to live in a town, I'll have them where they won't bother nobody. And where nobody will bother them."

"But then you love your snakes," said Father Savio.

"Well, sure I love them," said Calder defensively.

"But why?"

Calder saw that the priest's expression was one of genuine curiosity. He shrugged. "I don't know how to explain that. To me, they're the most beautiful things on God's earth. I'm not asking anybody else to understand that, no more than I want them to make me like the things they like."

Because he knew that the answer would somehow touch him, too, Father Savio asked the question with dread. "Haven't you ever been afraid of them?"

Calder looked a little past Father Savio's head. "I don't think so," he said. "But I can't be sure. I have got one, the big one, the brute, that's made me wonder sometimes. He's the most beautiful golden thing that ever lived, and I get to feeling that he knows me better than I know myself. I'm not afraid of him, and I like him more than any snake I ever had, but I don't understand him. He's got something about him that's always waiting, like he's God, and I got to keep him until I find out what it is."

Slowly, as Smale Calder spoke, the priest realized that he was seeing his first pure human being, without guise and without fear, as beautiful in his simplicity and as ugly as the very snakes he loved. Father Savio rose to his feet. "I have to tell you, Mr. Calder," he said. "No matter what you think of me for my part in this, I have to warn you of what is going to happen tonight."

Smale Calder regarded him querulously, like a child. His mouth framed to voice the question. It died stillborn with the hollow roaring in the night. Reading in the eyes of the priest the meaning of the sound, he stood up. Lurching to the door, he threw it open and saw the arc of light rising into the sky. He looked back once at the priest in final accusation, and then he was gone.

Father Savio followed him, calling incoherently into the night. A veil had begun to part in his soul, and with it had come the glimpse of an impending vision.

# 20

TWICE AFTER THE SUN HAD SET THE brute snake had come out of his cave and raised himself up to test the thickening dusk. He had cast from side to side with his great head, searching the air with the forked antenna of his black tongue. Each time he had retreated into the cave, to lie there looking restlessly out upon the quiet yard.

He made no sound until night had fallen, and then he began to rattle almost inaudibly for long periods of time. The other snakes had come out of their caves to laze on the white sand that held the day's warmth. But after a while his rattling began to affect them so that they, too, began to raise their heads in listening alert.

When the first shrouded sounds of movement in the night carried to the yard, the brute snake fell suddenly silent. He lay still as death until the sounds approached and entered the garage, and then he glided out of his cave. As he came onto the white sand, the other snakes made way for him, melting slowly back into the labyrinth of rocks from which they had come. He lay coiled and alone like a waiting sentinel until the big doors of the garage rumbled open, and then he raised himself up for the last time.

It was a moment before the men who came through the door could understand what they were witnessing. They peered in wonder at the apparition of the raised snake shimmering in the moonlight. There was a gasp, and someone said, "Will you look at that!"

Pasquale, who had led the way into the back yard, exclaimed with pride, "Santa Maria! He was waiting for us."

Amado had been at the rear of the group. He crowded into the front line. "He's a devil," he said in a shaken voice.

Even Della Santa had been struck silent by the aspect of the waiting snake. He roused himself when he saw that Giometti, who was standing beside him, had begun to quake so badly that the bucket he held was sloshing gasoline over its edges. Sensing a weakening in the resolve of the men, Della Santa said commandingly, "It is only a snake, after all. We came here to do a job. Now let's get on with it." He grasped Giometti's arm. "You first, unless you are afraid."

Giometti gaped at him, and then around at the others. Della Santa felt his arm harden with purpose. Pulling himself free, Giometti ran toward the snake pen, heaving out the contents of his bucket as he ran. The gasoline arched upward and fell in a cascade over the brute snake.

At the instant Giometti had begun to move, the brute snake lowered himself quickly into a coil. As the gasoline washed over him, he rattled piercingly. Giometti reeled backward, letting loose the bucket as if it were a snake itself. There was a guffaw from Pasquale, and then someone else laughed. In a moment, they were all laughing hysterically.

## 171 §

The tension was broken, and Della Santa began quickly to give orders.

"Soak down everything," he said. "The rest of them are hiding in the rocks."

The brute snake stood his ground until he had been doused many times over. Then he gave up and uncoiled and crawled ignominiously back into his cave. Giometti grew strong at the sight of his retreat, and called for everyone to see.

"Shut up, Giometti," said Della Santa, rapping his cane sharply on the garage door. "Don't stop for foolish things," he said to the men. "We have got to hurry before Calder comes back."

Giometti laughed menacingly. "What difference if he does come back? I told you I would take care of him."

But it was not Smale Calder that Della Santa was concerned about. Even if Calder had not been deceived by the ruse of the priest's summons, Giometti would have taken care of him exactly as he had promised. What Della Santa was really worried about was that Manuel Cafferata could still interfere. Joe Morelli had assured them otherwise when he came to the saloon, but there was always a chance that Cafferata might change his mind. If he did, he could regain the authority he had lost. Della Santa did not underestimate the chances of that. But when the snake pen was destroyed, so would be Manuel Cafferata's authority, once and for all.

Under Della Santa's prodding, the men moved more quickly, coming in repeated procession from the gasoline pump to the snake pen and emptying their buckets inside, until the air was choking thick with fumes. They soaked the rocks until they glistened in the moonlight, and even the white sand looked as wet as it did after a rain shower. When Della Santa judged that enough had been done, he called the men back into the garage and pulled the door shut.

"Give me the torch," he said. As agreed, he was to do the firing of the snake pen. Because he was not quite sure what would happen when he threw the torch, he hesitated, but only for an instant. There was no choice in the matter. He took the thin bundle of fagots through which an oil-soaked rag had been wound. "Light a match," he ordered.

The match flared in the darkness of the garage and moved toward the extended torch. Della Santa turned his head briefly as the torch burst into flame. When the flame subsided and was burning evenly, he gave the order to open the door. "As soon as I have thrown it," he said in a voice not altogether firm, "close the door as fast as you can. I have no wish to be burned."

As the garage door rumbled open, the men drew back until Della Santa was standing alone. Della Santa glared at them as at a desertion. Then he stepped into the open space and lofted the torch at the snake pen. He leaped back just in time to escape the big door's slamming home.

Even through the thickness of the wood, the heat and the rush of air jarred them like a blow. They waited silently, caught between a quick fright at what they had done and a fascination to see the end of it. Della Santa gave a command to open the door.

The snake pen was a pinnacle of flame in the night sky. The labyrinth of rocks and the white sand were consumed in fire that burned with the sound of hollow thunder. The heat was so intense that Della Santa was terribly afraid that they had gone too far, that in a moment the house and the garage and the fence would burst into flame, and that then the fire would go roaring through the town. He stood powerless to move until little tendrils of flame began to creep toward them along the paths where gasoline had dripped. He stamped at the nearest one and found his voice. "Put them out," he shrieked. "Put them out."

Shielding their faces with their arms, the men did as they were told. Then, as suddenly as it had leaped up, the fire began to subside until it was burning evenly in its confined space within the snake pen. The danger was past. Della Santa closed his eyes and leaned weakly on his cane. The thing was done, but it had been very close.

In the blindness of Smale Calder's going, the wooden gate had literally been burst apart. Because he had remarked upon it often as a thing of beauty fashioned with caring hands, Father Savio lingered beside its white ruin as if it were important. In one instant it had been an ordered entity. In the next, it was a mass of shattered fragments, and its beauty was destroyed forever.

There was shouting and crying in the night. In the fearfulness of the sounds, Father Savio remembered what he did not want to remember. He raised his eyes and saw the unnatural flare of light in the sky. Before he understood what he was doing, he was drawn through the open gateway and was running toward the source of what he did not want to see but that he knew he must.

The street that led to the garage was lined with women and children and old men who had come out of their houses. The children were wailing in fright, but their mothers could not break themselves away from the excitement in the night to take them inside. As the priest approached, an old man who had been given the duty caught at his arm with a bony grip. "Everyone must stay away!" he cried. The priest shook him off savagely and ran on between the lines.

When he came to the garage, he found his way blocked by the figure of Della Santa, who was trying to close the big doors. The banker had been manhandled. His tie was askew and his coat was torn, and he was pale with anger.

"You can't go in, Father," he said. "There is going to be fighting in there."

Father Savio nearly screamed. He raised his hand to strike the banker. Della Santa leaped back in surprise. Father Savio pushed his way past him.

"You will be sorry for this," cried Della Santa.

"You are right," Father Savio said. "I will be sorry."

He had expected violence when he burst through the garage into the yard. Instead, he found a silence so complete that it was unreal. The snake pen was a bed of blue fire that danced and fluttered with uncertain substance. It was ringed with a lurid circle of men, who stared into the flames as though they had been hypnotized. Mingled with the sweet odor of gasoline, there was a smell of burning flesh in the air.

Only Giometti had his back to the snake pen. His thick neck was bowed and his fists were clenched. Father Savio followed the direction of his menace and saw Smale Calder. He was standing like a broken ox. His shoulders were bent and tears were streaming down his cheeks. Someone beside him reached out a hand to touch him, and then drew it back hesitantly. It was Tony.

There was a murmur among the men, and a voice said, "Here comes another bunch."

Somewhere out of the burning labyrinth of rocks came crawling ribbons of fire. They came in one flurry of movement, as though they had been hiding together for safety until the reaching flames had driven them out. The gasoline had dripped down on them, and their backs were afire. They were making for the open patch of sand, but the rocks over which they came scorched their soft undersides, and they rolled more than crawled over the searing surfaces. Some fell into the crevices and died there, and one gray snake who ran the gantlet of fire was trying to leap into the air as though he had legs.

Those who made it to the sand came through the bed of fire with incredible swiftness to hurl themselves repeatedly at the wire fence. They died in agony. The rim of the snake pen was littered with their blackened coils.

Sickened, the priest turned away. A voice at his elbow said, "It's a dirty business, Father. But you must remember, it was your idea in the first place."

Della Santa had composed himself. His tie was straightened, and he was standing with both hands resting on his cane. He returned the priest's shocked gaze with vengeful containment.

Father Savio's protest was drowned out by Pasquale's cry of delight. "The big one's coming out. He's not dead at all."

The rocks that formed the brute snake's cave had burned like an inferno. It seemed impossible that he could have lived.

Yet now, in the dying flutters of flame, he emerged from his cave. He had been burning, and his great golden length was charred black. Still, his gliding movement did not reveal his suffering. It was deliberate and with purpose.

Giometti was caught unaware. Before he knew it, Smale Calder was tearing at the gate of the snake pen. With a roar of anger, Giometti moved to stop him. But even as he did, he was jolted off balance by a lunging body. Without even bothering to protect himself from the flailing blows, Giometti recovered himself and caught one of Tony's arms to hold him steady. There was a crunch of bone against flesh, and Tony was hanging in Giometti's grasp like a rag doll. Giometti raised his fist to hit him again. There was a shout, and then he remembered Smale Calder. But he was too late.

As Smale Calder approached, the brute snake drew himself into a coil. He waited until Calder had dropped to his knees and was reaching to pick him up, and then he struck him in the face. Calder sank slowly down on his haunches, and the brute snake struck him again. As though to make sure to himself that he had been bitten, Calder raised his hand to his cheek. Again, the brute snake curved back his head to strike. Calder made no move to escape. After a moment the brute snake uncoiled wearily, and Smale Calder opened his hands to receive him.

If he heard the shouts of the men begging him to come out of the snake pen, Smale Calder showed no sign of it. He might as well have been alone in the world with the brute snake. So unhearing were they in the solitude of their act that for no explainable reason the men fell quiet. Except for the slight forward drooping of Smale Calder's head as the poison began to creep into his heart, he and the snake could have been carved from stone.

Father Savio was crying. It was not from guilt but from a tenderness such as he had never known. He cried unashamedly until Smale Calder crumbled on his side and lay on the ground with the snake still held in the curl of his body. Then he walked to the gate of the snake pen.

There was a sharp call of warning from Della Santa, and the priest felt Giometti's big hands holding him firmly.

"A man is dying in there," said Father Savio.

"So what are you going to do," said Giometti. "Take the man away from the snake? Do you want to die, too?"

Della Santa stepped in front of the priest. "There is really nothing anyone can do, Father."

Father Savio disengaged himself gently from Giometti's grasp and looked about at the men. They were regarding him curiously. In the fading light of the flames, he saw Tony. The young man was white as death, and there was a great smear of blood on his cheek. The priest had expected hatred, and it was there, but suddenly as their eyes locked a wonder began to form in the young man's face.

Father Savio turned away and knelt on the ground. He raised his hand to his forehead. *"In nomine Patris . . ."*

"No, Father!"

His hand still raised, the priest paused in bewilderment. "Father, no!" Amado cried again. "You can't pray for him. The man was evil!"

And then, as the priest stared at Amado and saw mirrored the soul of his own shaping, the veil of his consciousness parted. The darkness of the night gave way to a brilliant vision of day and of the wheatfield of his dream, and in a white, numbing burst of clarity he saw at last the countenance of the man and recognized it for his own.

For a moment he thought that his heart had stopped and that he had died. The dream of the wheatfield was reaching out to claim him, and he knew that he was being drawn into it forever. Then he heard a voice imploring him, and he realized it was not from the dream. It seemed important that he should hear, but he could not make out the words. A hand touched him gently, and the touch reached into the depths of his being.

The vision began slowly to dispel. The world returned, and with it the night and the snake pen and the flames, and he remembered where he was.

He had thought the beseeching voice had been in his vision. But now he heard it beside him. When he turned, he saw that Tony was kneeling on the ground.

"Father, pray for him."

The priest heard the old words and knew that he had never really heard them before. So, after all, it had been as simple a thing as compassion. Straightening, he touched his hand to his forehead and began his prayer again.